AMPLIFIED

FICTION FROM LEADING ALT-COUNTRY, INDIE ROCK, BLUES AND FOLK MUSICIANS

AMPLIFIED

FICTION FROM LEADING ALT-COUNTRY, INDIE ROCK, BLUES AND FOLK MUSICIANS

★ Edited by Julie Schaper & Steven Horwitz ★

MELVILLEHOUSE
BROOKLYN, NEW YORK

AMPLIFIED

© 2009 Julie Schaper & Steven Horwitz

"Feed the Wife" by Zak Sally previously published in *The Recidivist*, La Mano Press, 2005

"Tender Til the Day I Die" previously published on fivechapters.com

Melville House Publishing
145 Plymouth Street
Brooklyn, NY 11201

www.mhpbooks.com

Boook design by Kelly Blair

ISBN: 978-1-933633-71-8

First Melville House Printing: March 2009

Library of Congress Control Number: 2009901635

For Enos and Nancy—
It all started with Tom Lehrer

TABLE OF CONTENTS

★

Amplified started with a question: Would the songwriter performers we listen to (alternative, alt country, Americana, roots, blues,
folk) be interested in writing short fiction?

We listened to a lot of music and made a lot of lists, went
on a yearlong CD buying spree, downloaded, and spent a lot of
time on musicians' websites. We talked to friends and got their
suggestions. We invited artists to join the project.

Whenever possible, we went to their shows. And at the end
of the evening, after the CDs were purchased and the auto-
graphs signed, we sat down with the artists. In some cases we
corresponded through email. We queried their management
companies. We received commitments, some warily and some
enthusiastically.

The result is *Amplified,* a collection of original fiction by
some of the most literate, eclectic songwriters working today.
We sought narrative songwriters who had never published or
had barely published fiction before but were willing to take a
chance—artists we thought *should* be writing fiction. And now
they have.

LAURA VEIRS

Several years ago we were on holiday in London. Solo artist Laura Veirs was playing at a club in the old Spitalfields Market. On our way to the show I realized that a pickpocket had stolen my wallet, so we spent the rest of the evening with the local constabulary in the underground. Since we missed her in person, we bought her wonderful CD *Carbon Glacier* and were intrigued by Laura's songwriting, particularly her many references to the natural world. In her story, "The Birdfeeder", an old man and a young woman's lives intersect in an unexpected way thanks to the odd intervention of nature.

CYNTHIA HOPKINS

We first saw Cynthia Hopkins in *Accidental Nostalgia,* a theatrical show she wrote and starred in, at the Southern Theatre in Minneapolis in January 2005. The performance included Cynthia's genre-bending band Gloria Deluxe,in a show the *New York Times* described as "avant-garde with a twang." We picked up *Hooker,* her second album, and we've been following her work ever since. Her story, "Quantum Gravity," is a memory piece about confusion, regret, and self-recognition.

CHRIS SMITHER

Chris is an American original—a solo artist who is a little New Orleans, a little Boston and a lot of road—and we've been listening to him for as long as he's been recording. "Leroy Purcell," his story about the odd relationship between a cop and a musician, is as accomplished and assured as his guitar playing. And that's saying a lot.

MARIA MCKEE

We became aware of Lone Justice at about the time that the band broke up and Maria started her solo career. The song "Panic Beach," from the eponymous first album, is a remarkably cinematic story, an arch tale of stalled stardom set in some small town on the vaudeville circuit. We knew that she could write. "Charcoal," her story in this collection, opens with a character saying, "I had a mystical experience with Johnny Cash's pants." What more can we say?

BEN WEAVER

Molly Maher, a musician in St Paul, MN, told us about this amazing solo artist Ben Weaver. We weren't familiar with his music. We bought a copy of his album *Paper Sky* and we were hooked. Ben's restless spirit is evident in everything he does—his art, songs, poetry, and fiction. *Mojo* has called him "a hillbilly Leonard Cohen."

CAM KING

I met Cam in Albuquerque in 1972. He was making short cowboy films, drawing comics, writing songs, and expounding passionately to anyone who would listen and to some who wouldn't about Jackson Browne and Sam Peckinpagh. He's been performing producing and writing ever since, most notably with The Explosives and the Freddie Steady 5. We are certain that after reading Cam's apocalyptic Texas tall tale, "Road Kill," you'll never be able to think about armadillos the same way again.

ROBBIE FULKS

Like a lot of listeners, the first time we became aware of solo artist Robbie Fulks was through what Steve Goodman called his "shtick-kicking" songs. It didn't take us long to realize that he was much more than just a wise-ass honky-tonk guy, although he is really good at it. Robbie reminds us of The Hanks. All of them. We wouldn't have been surprised if Robbie's story had been set on a dusty county road in rural Georgia. It's not, of course. The location is New York City and the story starts in a classroom at Columbia. Robbie never seems to be what he seems to be.

JIM WHITE

We're almost certain that we bought solo artist Jim White's *Wrong Eyed Jesus!* for the title but the music was a revelation. The liner notes included a great "true" story by Jim—we now take it as a sign that he was meant to do a story for us. "Pecan Trees Are Self Pruning" is a wry look at the nature of faith, belief and falling tree limbs.

RENNIE SPARKS

From the moment we picked up *In the Air*, we were captivated by The Handsome Family's dark and mysterious yet deceptively buoyant music. Reading Rennie's lyrics is like reading perfect flash fiction. Her story, "The Thicket," is work of surreal imagination, a cross between a Germanic fairy tale and an Appalachian murder ballad.

DAMON KRUKOWSKI

We've known Damon for years as founder, with Naomi Yang, of Exact Change, a press that publishes nineteenth and twentieth century experimental writers. We've listened to him for even longer, first as a member of Galaxie 500, then Magic Hour, and now as Damon of Damon & Naomi. "From Afterimage" is a meditation on memory and the brief moments that give our lives meaning.

PATTY LARKIN

Working on this book led to revisiting some of the music in our collection. Listening to some of solo artist's Patty Larkin's earlier music was all it took to remind us that she is a terrific songwriter and a formidable guitarist. Her latest CD only confirmed that opinion. Patty's story, "Baby Doll," is a testament to the goofy beauty of music and the capricious nature of the music business.

JON LANGFORD

I'm a sucker for seminal punk bands and the Mekons were it as far as I was concerned. It's hard not to be energized by lines like "destroy your safe and happy lives," something I was probably never going to do, but it felt pretty good singing along. Over the years, through The Waco Brothers and his solo work, Jon's music keeps changing and "safe" is still not part of his vocabulary. In his stunningly original story, "Inside the Whale," Jon creates a world in which the Great White and his sidekick Flipper the Dolphin swim the seven seas in a philosophical, literary, and vaudevillian search for meaning.

MARY GAUTHIER

We spoke with solo artist Mary Gauthier at the Cedar Cultural Center in Minneapolis after a show and asked her to contribute a story for the book. Mary said she couldn't write dialogue, but we reminded her that she wrote songs with dialogue—so why not a short story? In "The Holiday Inn Again," a precocious child navigates a life in which her parents are unable to be adults. People talk about authentic voices. Mary is the real deal.

ZAK SALLY

We've been fans of Low since we moved to the Twin Cities, but we didn't know about Zak's other life as a creator of comic books and impresario of La Mano Press until we started working on this book. We loved the idea of having a graphic work in the book and are delighted to have a piece from *The Recidivist*, Zak's self-published comic collection.

RHETT MILLER

We heard Terry Gross interview Rhett Miller on *Fresh Air* earlier this year and drove directly to The Electric Fetus and bought the latest Old 97's CD *Blame It on Gravity*.

Rhett's been writing smart lyrics for the band since it formed in 1993 and has a successful solo career as well. The story in this collection, "Tender Til the Day I Die" appeared on the website *FiveChapters*, and it appears here in book form for the first time.

DAVID OLNEY

Solo artist David Olney, formerly of the X-Rays, is widely known for his hardnosed blues, intense performances, and historical storytelling. It was his song about a religious huckster in *Jerusalem Tomorrow* that first got our attention and we've been listening ever since. David's story "A Sign from God" questions the mystery of God and the obsessive drama of religion. A lot has been written about Olney through the years but maybe the *Houston Press* said it best —"Olney stands out like a jalapeno in a bowl of vanilla pudding."

Leroy Purcell

★

BY CHRIS SMITHER

It's a boring drive from Houston to Dallas, and I felt lucky to have barely noticed the first half of it. ZZ Top at gain ten, cruise control at seventy-one, then an annoying flicker in the mirror that loomed with alarming speed into an action-mode police cruiser, lights going like a casino.

The cop was alarming too... maybe the biggest man I had ever seen up close, and he was very close, so close that his belt was two-thirds of the way up my window. I couldn't see any more of him until he bent over and looked through the windshield.

"How 'bout you step on out here," he said in a voice that sounded like it was all he could do to keep a leash on it, but was making an effort to do so. "Gotcher license and reg? Good, good, bring 'em on out."

Now, most cops on a highway stop don't want you out of the car, and if you try to get out they'll order you back into it. They like to keep you where you can't get at them, with your hands in plain sight. Once you get out of the car there's no telling what you might do, and even if you're gonna run they'd prefer you do it in the car. Cars are limited to certain kinds of terrain, like roads mostly, but a guy on the loose can go anywhere and probably will. Then they have to chase him and it's harder to call for help. It makes them tired and it makes them mad. Ordering someone out of the car is unusual and often a preliminary to an arrest, so I was apprehensive climbing out.

My first thought was "Goddamn it's hot," followed by "Goddamn this guy is big." He was at least six seven, and past that my estimates get unreliable, but the word that springs to mind is "towering." In his early fifties, heavy, too, but only a little bit in the way of fat, mostly just big hard stuff that fit together pretty well, maybe 275 lbs. Maybe more, I don't know, it wouldn't surprise me. The hand that he was holding out to me was the size of a dinner plate, but when I tried to put my license and the rental agreement into it he reached over and seized my other hand, gave it two hard shakes, and said:

"Leroy Purcell, Texas Department of Public Safety, how you doin' today?"

I mumbled something about how I'd been doing pretty well until just a minute or so ago when he jumped right in again, saying,

"Now, now, this ain't nuthin', this ain't gonna take but a few minutes an' we gonna have ya on yer way in no time. Come on back in the cruiser with me to where it's cool, we gonna get this all straightened out right away."

He opened the front passenger door for me then walked around to the other side. A Crown Victoria is not a small car, but I could feel it sag when he got in, and it felt almost cramped by the time he got himself arranged to his satisfaction and directed his attention to me. He reached over and indicated the radar readout with a forefinger like a Coney Island frank: "I gotcha dead to rights here, 71 in a 55 zone." Then he cocked his head almost quizzically. "Tell me, is they sumpin' goin' on here, some kinda emergency, sumpin' I should know about?"

It was delivered so perfectly, eyes wide with expectation, almost breathless anticipation in the voice, that the effect was comical in the extreme. In my experience it's never smart to laugh at anything a cop says, but I came close before saying that, no, I wasn't in any particular rush. Then I added: "Well, I do have a radio interview in Dallas at two." He made a show of looking at his watch, then nodded as though one of the world's great truths had just been confirmed. "It's gonna be a near thing," he said, "but I b'lieve you'll make it."

He had a roll-out keyboard under the dash, and he occupied himself for the next minute or so copying my license into the computer. Then...

"Holy smokes!" and this was the loudest I'd heard him yet. "Arlington, Massachusetts? You're not from Massachusetts, are yuh?"

God save me... John Kerry, Michael Dukakis, and Edward Kennedy were about to bury me deep on the lone prairie.

"Yes," I said, "That's my correct address on the license."

"But you're not from Massachusetts, are yuh?"

"Well, no, I wasn't raised there."

"Where was you raised?"

"New Orleans."

Leroy Purcell nodded again, indicating that perhaps yet another great truth of the world had surfaced. "I thought," he said ponderously, "that you sounded mighty polite for someone from Massachusetts."

For the next few minutes I had time to contemplate the array of equipment and weaponry in the car while Leroy finished up his "paperwork," all of which was done on the computer. Finally he handed me a stylus and a portable touch-screen pad.

"Just sign right there, and we'll getcha back on the road... Okay, just a second, this little thing's gonna printcha copy... there yuh go. Now you just call this number right here anytime between nine an' five, Monday through Friday, and they'll tell

you all you need to know about contestin' or payin' the fine.
Here's yer license an' all. Be careful pullin' out onto the highway,
there's crazies 'round here'll sneak up on you like a cat."

I thought I would risk a question.

"How much is this gonna cost me?"

"I wouldn't have the foggiest notion. I can't recall as I've
ever received a citation."

Well, no, I don't suppose so.

"How soon can I call to find out?"

"Just as soon as I push send," he said, and he did.

At a certain medium-to-low level in the music business, that is,
below the radar of mass circulation magazines and top-forty but
above playing in the subway, the radio interview is a constant
occurrence and is as essential to a continuing livelihood as, say,
maintaining a mailing list or having strings on the guitar. Nine-
ty percent of the stations that play the kind of music I make are
found below 92 on the FM dial, often sandwiched between a
couple of powerful signals selling god in one form or another.
These music stations love to have traveling musicians stop by for
a chat. It's a symbiotic relationship, with the additional appeal of
highlighting one of the principal differences between them and
the religious hucksters. As a DJ once told me, "Our persons of
interest actually show up once in a while."

I walked into the station in Dallas feeling a little poorer in
pocket, but armed with a story that was tailor-made for public
radio consumption. At a slight remove from the action it was
easy to highlight the funny parts and forget about the apprehen-
sion, so I played it for laughs and got plenty. The host of the
show was delighted, I got to sing a few songs, and I left feeling,
while not exactly benevolent, at least more kindly disposed toward law enforcement than I had been an hour earlier.

Leroy Purcell was outside the front door of the station, lean-
ing against his cruiser, cleaning his huge fingernails with a ludi-
crously small pen knife.

"Hey," he said. "I heard yuh on the radio."

There's a problem when it comes to talking to cops. I mean, you can't really talk to them, can you? You just never know how they're going to react. When I was a kid they scared me, but now most of them look like kids themselves... big kids with guns, and you don't know if they have a sense of humor. Sort of like big young dogs. They probably won't bite you, but you just never know. Leroy Purcell was no kid, but I didn't know if he was going to bite me or not. All I knew was that if he wanted to no one was going to stop him.

"I called that number on the citation," I said.

Leroy raised one eyebrow. Nothing else moved. A face like a ten-inch skillet and then this one eyebrow crawling up. It was unsettling, as though a face on Mt. Rushmore had suddenly winked. I'd love to be able to do that.

"You want to know what it's gonna cost me?"

He appeared to notice that his shoelace needed attention, so he raised a foot onto the hydrant he'd parked next to and farted prodigiously.

You see what I mean? There's just no talking to them.

"Two hundred and thirty-seven dollars," I said, while wondering how long he'd been saving his gastric disturbances and how he'd known he'd need them. Maybe it was like the eyebrow, just a talent he'd learned to exploit.

He decided his laces were satisfactory after all, so he put down his foot and said, "What time's yer show tonight?"

That was the last thing I'd expected him to say, but it's a question I'm so used to answering that I spoke up before it occurred to me to wonder why he wanted to know.

"I don't really know. I have to be there by about five-thirty for sound check, and I'll be there from then on. Probably around eight, eight-thirty. Depends on whether there's an opener." Then the oddity of it struck me, so I added, "Why? Have you got plans for me?"

"No, no, don't go gettin' yourself all snarled up now. This ain't nuthin' but a simple question," forgetting I suppose that the last time he'd said "this ain't nuthin" it had cost me two thirty-seven. "What's an opener?"

As Texans go, this one didn't seem to get out much.

"An opening act, someone who goes on first, usually no more than twenty or thirty minutes."

This was received with unblinking rumination for maybe fifteen seconds, then he turned quickly and yanked open the door to the cruiser.

"Okey-doke, have a good 'un."

I watched him drive off, and thought, "Shit." Then I thought some more and thought, "Well, shit." I hadn't been bit, but as Leroy might say, it was a near thing.

I was more or less out of sight in the backstage area waiting for the sound engineer to change the setup after the opening act when I saw him again. A lot of people saw him. It was people craning around to look at him that drew my attention, and of course he wasn't hard to spot. He'd changed into civvies, for which I was grateful, but it only diminished his impact a little. I watched him look around for a place to sit and pleaded silently with the powers that be to let him pick someplace out of my direct line of sight; the idea of playing a whole set looking right at him, or worse, with him looking right at me was more than I wanted to deal with. I needn't have worried. Even Leroy probably realized that sitting on a little plastic folding chair in the middle of that crowd was going to make him look like an elephant balancing on a bucket, so he sidled over and spread himself out generously over about half of one of the eight-foot pews that lined the wall. Still, he wasn't exactly hiding. He was most definitely there.

There's a semi-superstitious, emotional balancing act that fills the hour or so before a performance. Every artist handles it differently, but what they all have in common is a desire to avoid or hold at bay anything that might disrupt the flow, the progress, toward a sort of idealized state in which everything is both intense and effortless. When I approach that state I start to feel as though I'm both performer and audience; I have the luxury of listening to myself as a detached observer while at the same time experiencing a kinesthetic joy in the execution. It is the best drug, the smoothest high in the world, and it's legal. I get there maybe once in every twenty shows, and there was Leroy Purcell to make sure it didn't happen tonight.

I exaggerate, but that's how it seemed at the time. It takes a lot to really ruin a set though, and Leroy didn't come close. Shows take on a life of their own once they're started, and half of the time you find yourself straining just to keep up with things; no time to think, let alone pay attention to someone in your peripheral vision. I shot a look his way between songs once in a while, and never saw him move, or put his hands together, but that's not to say he didn't. I just never saw it. He didn't stand up at the end, either, though almost everyone else did, and that can require a conscious effort. If part of an audience stands up to applaud most of the others get up just to see over the crowd, whether they liked the show or not. Either way they get at least one more song.

For almost everyone the evening is over at that point, but it's just the beginning of the end game for me. There's a protocol involved in winding things up, including an appearance at the all-important merchandise table where the audience members can buy CDs, and, if they're willing to wait around, get them signed by the artist. Plus chit-chat. Plus reconciling the door money and the merch money. On a quick night it can take an hour, and if there are a lot of people buying and talking it can go longer. Still, I was a little surprised to see no sign of Leroy Purcell at the end of it. The surprise was short-lived. His car was next to mine, the two of them practically alone in the parking lot, and he climbed out of it as I approached.

"You never told me you was playin' in a church. This is a god-damn church!" his tone striking an unsteady balance between aggrieved and outraged. It set me back for a second, so I played for a little time putting down the gear and unlocking the trunk.

"Well," I said, "just barely. I think they're Unitarians. Besides," I added, "you were only in the annex, not the church itself. What's the matter with you and churches anyway?"

"I ain't hardly set foot in a church since I left home. Was all I could do to set still."

"That's okay," I said, inwardly marveling and a little frightened by the fact that we were having something that almost resembled a conversation. "I don't think most of the people in there tonight go to church any more often than you do. And if it weren't for church coffeehouses and church concert series I'd have a hard time making a living, and that's all there is to it. How'd you like the show?"

It took him a while to shift gears, and when he finally accomplished it he seemed to shudder like some giant machine that had suddenly dropped into neutral.

"The show? Yes, well, that'd be tough to say... I don't know the first thing about music."

I thought I would just let that one sit there for a while. That's something I've learned from both cops and shrinks. If you just wait, sometimes you'll get more information without having to risk a dumb question. Leroy was familiar with the technique, too, and I could see he didn't like having it turned around on him one little bit. He half-turned to get back in his car, then thought better of it and turned back with his hands jammed in his pockets.

"Listen," he said in an unnecessary whisper since there was no one within a hundred yards of us, "I need you to do sumpin' fer me."

You see? This is where I could have really used that eyebrow crawl, but I didn't have it. Just had to sit there and do my best to project a stony silence.

"I got a tape I wantcha to listen to. Sumpin' I want yer opinion on."

"A tape?" I said, "What kind of tape?"

"Well, it ain't really a tape. It's more like a disc, a whaddya call it, a CD."

"You mean a music CD?"

"Well of course ... songs, like what you do."

"Let me get this straight. You want my judgment on some music even though you don't know enough about music to tell whether or not my opinion is worth anything. Have I got that right?"

With that his whole demeanor changed. He'd been a little embarrassed, but now his confident, easy manner re-appeared and he looked at me almost pityingly.

"I don't need to know anything 'bout music. I been watchin' people at their work all my life. It don't matter what they're doing, I can tell inside of five minutes if a man knows how to do his job. You're good at what you do; don't try to tell me different."

It was ridiculous, the whole situation, and the worst of it was that I could feel myself flushing because in many ways it was the richest compliment I'd ever received, precisely because it wasn't intended as such. I coughed and cleared my throat to cover my embarrassment.

"So you're saying that you want to engage my services as a consultant?"

"I just want you to listen to this and tell me if it's any good. Does it have any merit at all? Is it worthwhile?"

"I understand that. Normally I get paid for that kind of work."

"So how much would that kind of work cost?"

I took a deep breath and tried to keep my voice steady. "Two hundred and thirty- seven dollars."

I thought he'd surely seen it coming, but he hadn't and it blindsided him. A brief look of what could only have been rage flicked across that normally impassive face and disappeared immediately.

"Okay, okay, I'll make the citation go away. Just forget about it, toss it."

I shook my head slowly. "No, I'll deal with the ticket. You got me fair and square. I just want the money to come from you."

He looked hard at me. "What d'you care? You think I deserve a fine?"

"Maybe not a fine exactly, but I'd like to think that the next time someone asks you how much a ticket costs you'll remember."

He stood there for a few seconds looking past me at nothing. Then he made a little sucking noise through his front teeth. "Okay, smart guy, you gotcherself a deal. When can you listen to it?"

"I have to drive to San Antonio tomorrow. I'll listen in the car in the morning. Give me a number or an address and I'll let you know what I think."

"No, that's alright. I'll find you. Sometime in the afternoon."

I thought to myself, "Shit," as he started climbing into his car, and then I said, "Bring a check," as he closed the door and drove off.

I got on the road the next morning about ten, and as soon as I was comfortable on the interstate, big coffee situated in the cup holder, I stuck the CD in the player on the dash. There were only four songs on it, and by the time I was almost to Waco I'd probably listened to it half a dozen times. Then I turned it off and drove in silence for almost an hour.

There's a whole genre of American folk songs that are collectively grouped under the heading of "murder ballads." Some of them have even become pop hits, for instance, "Tom Dooley" or "Frankie and Johnny," and one of the peculiarities that many of them have in common is that they don't make a lot of sense. You get a song about a guy who's crazy in love with some doe-eyed maiden, so he takes her up a mountain and stabs her to death. Or shoots her. Then he comes back home and gets himself hanged. Poor boy. End of story. No rhyme or reason, no explanations. They must have been wildly popular at some point, because there are so many of them and I guess they still are in some way, because people still sing them.

What I was listening to were four contemporary murder ballads, and they were as compelling as anything I'd listened to in a long, long time. Think about Randy Newman when he's completely subsumed into one of his untrustworthy characters; you start to see the situation clearly, but from an alien point of view, and it gives you the creeps because you realize that it makes sense in a way that you would rather not believe you were capable of understanding. This was like that, all in the first person, all delivered in a smooth low-tenor voice that could have been soothing if you weren't paying attention to the horrific content. One of the songs was a cappella; the other three were accompanied on guitar, and nicely. Nothing fancy, but competent, with good time, and nothing to distract from the story. Stories to make you wish they'd give you some relief, but were relentless and inescapable. I was exhausted.

I was starting to feel a little disoriented, too, so I pulled off the highway just shy of Temple and started looking for somewhere to go in and sit down for a while. All I remember of the outside are two dusty gas pumps and a sign that read EAT B'FAST, LUNCH, DINER. I sat down at a booth, ordered coffee, and stared unseeing at a menu until I heard the screen door screech and slam. Leroy Purcell walked over and sat down across from me, and it's a measure of how strange I was feeling that I didn't think to wonder how he'd found me; I was just glad to see him.

"You lookin' a little puny," he said. "How you feelin'?"

"I've been better. I expect I'll be better again soon, and I've got some things I'd like to know that could help me get there, like where you got these songs for instance."

The waitress came over with my coffee just then and asked him if he wanted some. He nodded and asked for pie as well, and it was my turn to nod and say, "Yeah, me too." Leroy watched her walk away and then turned back to me.

"I'm the one who needs the help. Id'n that what the deal was?"

That was indeed the deal, and I had to admit to myself that I had taken on the job in the smug certainty that the songs would be routinely awful, that I could pick from a dozen stock criticisms I'd developed over the years and be done with it. Now it appeared I was going to have to do some work. Actually think about what I said. So I did. Just sat there and thought about it, and when Leroy started to say something I held up a hand without looking at him until he settled back down in his seat. Finally I took a big slug of the coffee and put the cup carefully back on its saucer.

"Here's what I think," I said. "Apart from the subject matter, which is a whole other thing, this stuff is as good or better than ninety-nine percent of what's out there right now. By 'out there' I mean material being played day in and day out by journeyman musicians and singers a lot like me who are making a living at what they do. Believe me, in this world at this time that's saying a lot, even though none of them are household names by any stretch of the imagination. Don't ask me if it's good, because 'good' has a lot of funny connotations that might not apply here, but is it valid? Yes. Is it worthwhile? Yes. It's extremely well done by someone with a lot of talent, and I would really like to meet him, even though the thought of it scares the bejeesus out me."

When I'd finished Leroy just sat there nodding his head and making that little sucking noise through his front teeth. Then he took a breath and blew it out slowly before he spoke.

"No need to concern yourself about that, 'cause it ain't gonna happen. He ain't in no condition to entertain visitors."

"What?" I said. "Is he sick?"

"Oh, he's plenty sick alright. He's fixin' to die."

"Oh man, of what?"

"Lethal injection, leastways if nobody else gets to him first. They's plenty would love the opportunity. They got him over to Huntsville."

The look on my face was all the answer I could muster, and I guess it was enough for Leroy. After a bit he spoke again.

"Listen," he said. "This is a really bad man, bad like you never want to know about, let alone go associatin' with. He's killed a lot of people and caused more trouble and grief than you would think possible. I've known him off and on his whole miserable life, and I ended up arrestin' him. What you just told me is the first, the only positive thing I have ever heard in connection with him, and I have no doubt it will be the last. This is a guy who watches TV coverage of the people marchin' outside the prison with signs for and against executin' him, and he identifies with the ones who want him dead. Says they're the only ones who understand what it's like to be him, to have an overwhelming desire to kill someone. Don't waste your time worryin' 'bout him. All you should be thinkin' is that you've earned your money."

With that he slid an envelope over to me and stood up. Halfway to the door he stopped and turned back to me.

"Thanks for the coffee, and speakin' of associatin', you should steer clear o' them churches. I know you think you're takin' advantage of 'em, but in my line of work you see firsthand what hangin' out with the wrong kind of people can lead to, and them frauds ain't gonna do you a lick of good. If the kind of god they talk about was even half real I'd be out of a job, but as it is I'm as close to bein' god as anyone in six counties is ever likely to see. If that don't scare the shit out of you, you ain't half as smart as I think you are."

That was the last time I saw Leroy Purcell.

Except that it wasn't. Well, it was and it wasn't. The next morning I was in the San Antonio airport, having worked the night before in one of the places Leroy warned me about. Not enough sleep, but I didn't really care. I would be unconscious for the next four hours on the nonstop back home. I was sitting at the gate with a half-hour until boarding, thumbing through the paper when I saw his picture. Or thought I did. I read the story.

Dauphin Purcell, age twenty-nine, convicted of four homicides and suspected of six others over a ten year period, had been executed by lethal injection just after midnight. He'd refused his last meal and had spent his last hours in prayer with his mother, an ordained minister. The last paragraph of the article indicated that Dauphin Purcell was the largest man ever executed in Texas, causing some uncertainties as to the dose required to kill him. It was resolved apparently; he was pronounced dead at 12:06 A.M. I got on my plane and managed to stay awake all the way home.

Charcoal
★
BY MARIA McKEE

"I had a mystical experience with Johnny Cash's pants," she said
without a modicum of irony. Elizabeth watched as the woman
twirled her luminous moon-white hair into an immense rope
and draped it to one side of her neck. "I was working as curator
for the costume department of the country music museum in
Nashville. We were getting ready for a big exhibit that upcom-
ing week and I was working quite late. I was fitting a form with
one of Johnny Cash's suits, one he'd worn very early on in his
career. So early, in fact, that this particular suit had been hand
sewn by his mother." She spoke in a low dulcet tone, almost
monotone, the words marched out in rapid succession the way
people with excess knowledge tend to express themselves. Not
so much to make a connection, but to clear the decks. To make
room for more. "As I hung the jacket on the form, I straightened
the shoulders and ran my fingertips along the underside of the
lapels, much as you would for a husband or a partner, you know,
getting ready to go out for an evening. A very familiar, a very intimate gesture between two people. I've never been married, but
anyway, as I lined up the creases in the pant legs and smoothed

out the metallic braid along the outside seam, I remembered the drum majorette suit that I wore as a little girl in Texas with that exact same braid hand-stitched by my mother."

They'd all been in the bar at the Warwick for a good few hours. People were feeling the time, the wine had been flowing. Elizabeth had engaged in several rather heady conversations with the various members of the group and had managed to hold her own. Though not an artist herself, she was used to keeping company with other artists and their colleagues, mostly tagging along with her best friend Finn. They'd met at Trinity College in Dublin twenty years earlier. He had thought she was ridiculous. A Goth hippie from Beverly Hills. But now that their friendship had spanned decades and continents, she believed nobody on earth knew her better, including her ex-husband. Finn had become an important sculptor now and was being feted accordingly. He spoke brilliantly and held court, but to Elizabeth he would always be someone with whom to practice scatological wit and binge eat.

"Isn't there a Dr. Seuss story about a pair of pants alive with nobody inside them?" Finn shouted at Elizabeth, who often served as his memory keeper. Before Elizabeth could reply, the woman with the long moon-white hair toned in, voice like a cello,

"'The Pale Green Pants.' I could recite it by heart as a very small child. My mother used to love to bewilder dinner guests by telling them that I could read perfectly before the age of three then sit me down with the book and have me retell the story from memory. When in fact the only advancement I had prodigiously acquired was the early propensity to horde useless information, among other things!" As they all laughed, the person whom Elizabeth could only identify to herself as "the woman who had done a lecture on Anton Mesmer and the Mesmerist cult" grabbed the woman with the moon-white hair by the arm and gasped, "Yes! The pale green pants are just as terrified of us as we are of them!"

"Don't they actually weep bitterly at one point in the story?" Finn snickered. He was wearing a hat that made him look like a middle-aged Peck's Bad Boy.

The husband of the woman who had been introduced earlier that evening to Elizabeth as "the medical director of the first family planning clinic in Ireland" shouted over the laughter to the woman with the moon-white hair, "Wait, what about your story? So what happened? You were communing with the metallic cord on Johnny Cash's pants, then what?"

"Well, I felt a male presence. Very strong, very male. A male ego. A deep, deep shudder. It went right through me. A distinctly large and unmitigatedly male presence".

"Wow," said the manchild Elizabeth could only identify just then as her best friend, but had for the moment forgotten his name. "Was it sexual?"

"No, not at all. But sensuous. Intercessional. Intimate. More intimacy than I've felt, possibly, ever." Elizabeth turned to speak, but couldn't. It was as if her mind and the inside of her mouth were connected by a great white beam of light that could make no shadows, no matter how her tongue and brain tried to connect. The beam of light was impenetrable. It startled her. Finn noticed. "You okay? You wrecked? Want me to get you a cab?" She opened her mouth, but nothing came out. She tried again, nothing. She must have looked like a little fish, opening and closing her mouth, eyes perplexed. Finn giggled, bemused, "What's wrong with ya!" Then suddenly, almost involuntarily, she sang out in a clear, confident, and strident tone:

"It's true no greater love at last
has found the maid with moonlit tresses
who in the pants of Johnny Cash
has found all that heav-en possesses..."

Elizabeth had never been musical. She couldn't play a note and refused to sing in public. Until now, but was that even her? The vigor of that voice had frightened her. The melodies and the tones were exotic and complicated. She looked around the room at the acquaintances, half expecting their attention to be on somebody else. But it was all on her. The group was applauding her robustly and laughing and calling out. "Are you drunk?" Finn was beside himself, chortling and wincing at her in disbelief. He knew she only drank a glass or two of wine, then got a headache. It had always been that way. For twenty years. She didn't get drunk. Some people just don't. She wasn't drunk now.

"Perhaps I was just very moved, that's all. Compelled by the odd and reverent tale of the woman with the long moon-white hair," thought Elizabeth as she opened her mouth to tell Finn that "of course she wasn't drunk," but instead she was seized by another paroxysm of song:
"Perhaps the vaunted man in black
has made a pilgrimage to send
a muse to strike a chord, alas
to bless your humble tone-deaf friend..."
Elizabeth held the last note and her strange new voice caught and caressed it until it formed extravagant shapes. Finn shouted over the din made by the cheering acquaintances. "What's come over you? Have you completely lost your marbles?" Elizabeth was reticent to respond. The swollen beam that was blocking her speech was still there. Then, just like that, it heaved and burst apart. She spoke, but all she could say to Finn was, "I don't know."

After a moment when the party had quieted some, the woman whose beatific story had inspired such a peculiar event came around the table and sat beside Elizabeth on the sofa. "I've been wanting to get a closer look at your rings all evening. May I?" she asked as she held out her hand to Elizabeth. Her fingers were long and milky white like her hair.

"Oh yes, of course", Elizabeth replied, "I've been collecting antique mourning jewelry for years. I can never decide which

ones to wear, so I put them all on. But this one is my favorite."
She held out her pinky and on it a small gold engraved ring with
a tiny portrait of a human eye painted on ivory under glass. "The
Lover's Eye," said the moon woman, "King George the Third
had a mistress named Maria Fitzherbert. She sent him a jeweled
portrait of her eye in secret. Of course the secret got out and a
fashion for 'eye jewelry' was propagated in the mid nineteenth
century. Oh look at this one!" she said fondling Elizabeth's ring
shaped like a coiled snake set with ruby eyes. "When I was a
young girl I wanted so badly to be transformed into Medusa. I
would lay awake on my bed at night and stare at the strands of
my hair draped across the pillow and will each strand, with all
my might, to move." Elizabeth felt the urge to sing again, but
just managed to stifle it. She grabbed the moon woman's pallid
hand and tried to speak but the blocking beam was back. She
squeezed the woman's hand gently and searched her eyes. The
woman searched back, warmly. "I come across these rings now
and again in my travels. Give me your email address. I'd like
to keep in touch with you anyway. I've always wanted a friend
with an ability to compose a light-hearted aria for any occasion!"
Laughing, she pulled her hand away from Elizabeth, who was
still gripping it quite strongly, and retrieved a pen and business
card from her handbag. Elizabeth took the pen and card and
put pen to paper, but found she could not write. Furtively, she
slipped the business card back in the moon woman's handbag
unmarked.

Elizabeth worked in her hometown of Beverly Hills as a
sometime associate producer of films that were often more chal-
lenging and interesting than the typical Hollywood dross, but
it was basically a glamorous bookkeeping job. She'd grown up
a bit spoiled and never attracted a particular work ethic. She
was mostly held aloft professionally by all the friends she'd met
and made through her ex-husband, a well-respected and intelligent director. She'd been too smart to become an actress, not

ambitious enough to produce and not talented enough to write or direct. She loved the movies, but only wanted to work with people she liked. That suited her fine. She didn't enjoy being too busy. She'd taken care of a brilliant and impossible man for many years. And, she had loved him. All she really wanted to do now was read and travel.

When Elizabeth returned from her trip to New York, she slept more than usual, dreaming vividly. In one dream, she visited a parallel universe where matter spontaneously erupted. Buildings imploded, parked cars crashed in on themselves, people awoke from sleep with bruises and swelling and missing teeth. She wandered the torn-up streets in acute physical pain, familiar landmarks in various stages of demolition. She saw her ex-husband pass but he didn't know her and she couldn't reach him.

A few weeks passed without incident. Elizabeth attributed her bizarre behavior that night at the Warwick Hotel to jet lag. Travel stress. Perimenopause. She tried not to think about it. It embarrassed her gravely. Then one night at the symphony, she felt a familiar detachment from her own body. She had gone with some friends to the Disney to hear a favorite Vaughn Williams piece. As the orchestra played, she saw the music in shapes and colors as vividly as a photograph. The images interacted with one another and with the music cohesively. The images were distinct and iconic, but unfamiliar. A new lexicon of symbols and vistas. She nearly lost consciousness, but the piece finished and the applause broke her reverie. She didn't speak for an hour after the concert finished. The blocking beam was back. Her friends didn't seem to notice. They knew her well enough to navigate her moods and they also knew how passionate she was about Vaughn Williams. She began to wonder, "Could I be breaking down?" She locked it away.

Elizabeth was between jobs and in no hurry to get back to work. She read, watched old films, hiked, went to the beach and to museums, and saw friends for dinner. Nothing untoward. She was glad to be home. The city looked different after her trip to New York. Cleaner, brighter. She saw things she'd taken for granted as if she were seeing them again for the first time. The intricacies of the Spanish ironwork. The bougainvilleas and bird of paradise. The art deco facades and towering palms. She drove her car up onto the curb on Santa Monica Boulevard because she was gawking at the cactus garden beside The Good Shepherd Church. A spot she'd passed almost every day, apart from her years abroad and in New York, for over forty years.

She holed up at home, did some gardening, and cleaned out all her drawers and closets. She gave away bags of stuff, then shopped for more. She redecorated a little. One day she was perusing interior design blogs and magazines when she came across an article about an elderly French sculptor who decorated her cottage in Vence with naïve drawings sprawled out across the sun drenched plaster walls in sepia charcoal. They were whimsical and childish and stirring. Elizabeth went into her minimalist dining room and stared at the white wall. The French doors opposite bathed the wall in a pale golden wash, typical of a clear early spring evening in Los Angeles. She stood and stared at the wall until the room dimmed then darkened with the hours.

The next morning she awoke early and went to an artist supply store. She bought several boxes of charcoal and pastel implements in varying shades of brown, gray, and black. Back home in the dining room, she started at the base of the wall opposite the French doors. She covered space in good time, stopping only to visit the toilet and drink water. When night fell, she blared up all the lights and continued. Every five hours or so she would shuffle distractedly into the kitchen, take out a carton of yogurt and suck it down without tasting it. When she began to feel hot, she discarded articles of clothing as needed, tossing them out into the hallway. By mid-afternoon the next day she had finished the wall and was dragging a stepladder out of the garage to start on the ceiling. She could hear bells ringing and tones going off vaguely as if through a tunnel. Voices on an answering machine the only one she heard was Finn's. "Where are you? Why haven't you called me back? You left some garbled message about St. Paul de Vence. Are you in the South of France? Should I worry? Call me, you lazy fat ass!"

After six days, there was no wall or ceiling space left. Elizabeth had gone through five boxes of charcoal and her fingers looked as if she had been clawing coal out of a mine with her bare hands. She stood back and looked at the dense images that covered every visible inch of the room. The drawing was as masterful and competent as a da Vinci sketch, with a dizzying command of realism and attention to detail. The centerpiece was a huge Medusa head, the roiling snakes spinning around her exquisite face rendered with terrifying anatomical precision. There was a life-size, lifelike portrait of a young Johnny Cash, brandishing a guitar and scowling, his trousers covered in a dozen or so human eyes that wept tears which fell in streams under a photolike image of the Liffey Bridge in Dublin and O'Connell Street. There was a drawing of Elizabeth and Finn as they looked in college, young and soft and wearing too much eye makeup, ragged black clothes, and Dickensian hats. On the ceiling was a giant Goya-esque portrait of an eighteenth-century noblewoman holding an oversized open locket in the palm of her hand. Inside the locket was a portrait of her eye, and reflected in the eye was the same image of the noblewoman holding an oversized open locket in the palm of her hand, with a portrait of her eye inside the locket. There were images of her ex-husband as Jupiter and herself as Semele, there were vines and birds and tiny Bosch-like creatures, musical notations, and snatches of poetry. Even the floor had scrollwork designs edging out from the mural like a rococo frame. Elizabeth spun slowly on her bare feet blinking, and looking up and around. She was breathing heavily and opening and closing her mouth looking to form words again, like that little fish from before. The blocking beam burst apart in sparks and she could speak. She said out loud, her voice rough and scorched, "I think... I think... I'm finished." Her bare heels slipped away from her and she collapsed, dead weight, to the floor.

She awoke at UCLA hospital to find out she'd been in a coma for days. The maid had found her in a heap on the dining room floor. Her naked body was smeared with dark muddy streaks and her lips and tongue were black. She was very badly dehydrated. Her ex-husband was sitting beside her on the bed. "I always knew you were extraordinary," he said. She couldn't speak, but if she could she would have said that a comment like that was symbolic of everything that was wrong with the marriage. "Finn's flying out. He had to stop in New York first, but he'll be here in a day or so. Of course he's been calling nonstop." She stared at him conspiratorially. He must know that she had lost the ability to speak because he hadn't asked her any questions, like, "How do you feel?" Or, "Can I get you anything?" Instead, he continued nervously as he took her hand. "Okay, so here's what's going on. It's not malignant, but I guess you have some sort of brain tumor and they're going to keep you here for a while and then take it out. It's very rare. Of course I'd expect nothing less from you". He winked and squeezed her hand. "Anyway, you're going to make into the text books. Apparently it was causing some sort of dementia and something called 'aphasia.'" She turned her head away. Tears ran down her cheek. She was whispering something hoarsely. Her ex-husband put his arms around her. "What darling? What is it?"

"Charcoal... charcoal... charcoal... charcoal..." She said it over and over until her voice gave out and she could only mouth the word. She couldn't stop. A quarter of an hour went by. He stroked her head until she fell asleep.

Elizabeth very nearly fully recovered, although it took quite some time. Her diagnosis of frontal lobe dementia gave plenty of mileage to Finn, who now called her "full frontal mental." The mural wasn't a dream or figment of her imagination; it remained there in her dining room in all its strident glory. Of course it had been promptly recorded and photographed by several psychiatric and neurological journals. After the initial awe surrounding it had died down, it became little more than a conversation piece. It made Elizabeth uncomfortable and she no longer liked to entertain in the dining room, but instead set up a table in the drawing room, "Like they do in New York," she told herself.

Finally she found she could no longer bear to live with the mural but couldn't bring herself to be the one to destroy it. Although Finn protested with tears, she decided to sell the house and move. A wealthy Bohemian couple from Antwerp bid well above the asking price. They were intrigued by the lore associated with the mural, but unfortunately it did not comply with the very strict brief executed by the important designer they had hired to do a revision of the house, so it would have to be, regretfully, removed. They had, however, arranged for a photo essay of the mural to appear in *World Of Interiors* magazine with a text written by Marie-France Boyer. Although Elizabeth and all her friends were fans of *World of Interiors* magazine, she thought it best to decline an interview and refused to be named in the story.

Inside the Whale
★
BY JON LANGFORD

We saw a better world just around the corner
Time's arrow pointing down some happy trails
Big clear dreams arising over the event horizon
But no light escapes
From inside the whale

Long blue summer nights, some basic human rights
The lunar landing craft, a donkey's ear and tail
All swallowed up as midnight struck
It's so dark down here
Inside the whale

An end to hunger, equality, under the sea
Inside the whale

Progress, progress, rose tinted glasses
cock-eyed optimism all cracked and paled
And all the astronauts and the Kennedys got caught
Down in the depths
Inside the whale

So naïve, this white boy's dream
Tucked up in bed
Inside the whale

Dolphin Information Age

It was the dolphin who told me about the old sea Captain and all the fuss you people made. I have to say it didn't ring any bells at all. Dolphins are really smart, smarter than you could ever imagine. This one had read the book from cover to cover and when she finally bumped into me (literally colliding with my scarred white flank somewhere off the west coast of Africa!) she could scarcely believe it. She never even saw me (so much for that mighty dolphin sonar!).

She said you'd been looking for me forever. How was I supposed to know? "You're most famous," she clicked. "You're bloody mythic," she added with a frantic nodding screech. Apparently, I discovered, I am the very rarest stuff of legend. This Dolphin knew everything. She even knew my name, which was, of course, at that time, still unknown to me. Dolphins don't have names; they're way beyond all that. So we'll just call her Flipper.

The First Return to the Deep

Like me, she ditched dry land hundreds of generations ago. The time was right. All that earthly tattle and crap was weighing her down, the gravity of it all depressed her. With every hailstone and pecan nut that fell and cracked her rapidly expanded mammalian skull she inched deeper into the wetlands before finally shedding her fur and feet to slip back beneath the waves forever. Too much responsibility. It was the only intelligent thing to do. Who has the will to stay grounded when right next door the neighbors are frolicking in the pool?

But even as she soared through the warm bright bubbly blue Flipper still nursed a hankering for that old abandoned world of dust and roots and shale. She was endlessly curious and could never resist exposing her smooth gray beak to the dry air above and taking a peek at what you lot were up to. A dangerous game indeed, for as she told me there are waves in the air which are pretty much the same as the waves in the sea except a terrible monster has clogged them all up with his pictures and numbers, his bleeps, lies, and messages of doom. That's probably why Flipper's sonar went haywire and I'm washed up on this mud bank.

Crap Book Review #1
This is an ill-compounded mixture of romance and matter-of-fact. The idea of a connected and collected story has obviously visited and abandoned its writer again and again in the course of composition. The style of his tale is in places disfigured by mad (rather than bad) English; and its catastrophe is hastily, weakly, and obscurely managed . . . The result is, at all events, most provoking book—neither so utterly extravagant as to be entirely comfortable, nor so instructively complete as to take its place among documents on the subject of the Great Fish, his capabilities, his home, and his capture. Our author must be henceforth numbered in the company of the incorrigibles who occasionally tantalize us with indications of genius, while they constantly summon us to endure monstrosities, carelessnesses, and other such harassing manifestations of bad taste as daring or disordered ingenuity can devise. . . . We have little more to say in reprobation or in recommendation of this absurd book. . . . Mr. Melville has to thank himself only if his horrors and his heroics are flung aside by the general reader, as so much trash belonging to the worst school of Bedlam literature—since he seems not so much unable to learn as disdainful of learning the craft of an artist.
—Henry F. Chorley, in *London Athenaeum*, October 25, 1851

Flipper agrees with the man from the *Athenaeum*. She liked the movie better. She's been reading the book to me for years, bit by bit (from memory of course), and she's pretty sick of it. She only perseveres because I'm in it. One day, she hopes, it will all come back to me. I find it totally impenetrable. We wonder if anybody in the world has ever sat down and read the whole thing straight through. I can't really tell if the mad (rather than bad) English belongs to the book or if it's just Flipper's translation. Dolphins do have an accent and the constant retelling of this story may have added some weird Chinese whisper filter that's distorted its whole factual basis beyond all recognition. Maybe it wasn't really me? Maybe it wasn't a whale at all?

Sometimes we stop reading the book and make up our own versions. They are usually shorter and funnier:

One cold Christmas night the grumpy, obsessive manager of the Peapod vegetarian restaurant is sitting all alone. He's watching re-runs of Matlock on his tiny black-and-white TV and eating a stale alfalfa sprout sandwich when he hears someone knocking very lightly on his front door. There's a blizzard raging outside and as he opens the door thick flakes of snow come blowing into the restaurant and stick to his eyebrows and beard. He looks back and forth but can't see anyone and he's about to shut the door when a tiny voice says, "I'm down here!" He looks down and sees a white snail on his doorstep. "Hello and Merry Christmas," says the white snail. "Can I come in and share some of your Christmas cheer? It's very cold out here and I have nowhere to go." The manager of the Peapod picks up the white snail and throws him as far as he can out into the freezing snowstorm. One year later, on Christmas night, he's still alone, watching the same TV show and eating what's left of another stale old sandwich. Suddenly he hears someone knocking and once again when he opens the door there's nobody there. He peers out into the blizzard and is just about to shut the door when a tiny voice from down below says, "What did you do that for?" The end.

Flipper used to tell one about Ray Bradbury going into a Starbucks, but I don't get it.

Migration Fatigue

"You got to keep moving, Blondie," screeches Flipper, just as I'm nodding off. She swims round and round my hump in neat concentric spirals leaving a trail of perfect little bubbles in her wake. "There, I confess, a nice halo for Virgin Whitey! Ha ha! Wakey,

wakey! Can't stop now." I know, I've trudged round this planet's oceans for nearly two hundred years and I'm ready to retire. Where the hell are we anyway? Flipper thinks you should never travel by the same route twice. "Think up new ways always, new directions, fire up the dry bone synapses," she says. "Drive that car home from work the same way every night and you'll be getting brain rot then crash, wallop, dead!" She looks down her beak at all the millions who journey as slaves to instinct, hunger, and yearnings.

The Filming of *Moby Dick* in Youghal
Death to Moby Dick signed Gregory Peck
In and out of his make-up
With a whale-bone for a leg
And the little bar down by the quayside
Was a goldmine everyday
Just like sitting on an oil-well
When the motion picture people came to stay

White whaler, big heart
Out there hunting with the hounds
Caught much more with a camera
Panned across the faces of the people hanging round
So all the local were extras and all the locals got paid
There's no acting in the flat black eyes
Of old women as the Pequod sailed away

40 summers dived out of reach
And on a TV round the back
We've got a picture on a videotape
Of the big fish that never came back
So far from the heart of Europe
The young left long ago
To look for work in London
Boston and Chicago

In 1954 we went on a trip to the Irish Sea, just Flipper and me. There's a little port town just east of Cork called Youghal where John Huston the famous Hollywood movie director was making a film of the book. He wanted to film it there so he could go fox hunting on his days off. It was a long way for us to go for a movie but Flipper was still a pretty good navigator back then. An actor called Gregory Peck played the old Captain, tottering around on a fake whalebone leg looking more like Abe Lincoln than anyone else. Flipper says Peck is the perfect name for an actor who plays a man who is in fact an egg with a baby chick inside.

We swam fairly aimlessly just outside the harbor walls and nobody ever spotted us. Not even when I was lying there logging in the warm Gulf Stream waters during those long boring gaps between takes. That was the first time I noticed that shiny thing stuck through Flipper's fin. She caught me staring at it through the snot-green seawater. "Don't worry, Snow-cone, it's germ-free."

I never found out who they got to play me. That was all done somewhere else. The crew and cast all stayed at Paddy's Hotel and signed publicity photos for Paddy the owner who had them mounted and framed and hung on the wall of the bar to remind everyone who came in for a drink that this was the last thing that was ever going to happen in that town.

Flipper says Paddy got it all wrong and things in Youghal are definitely on the up and up. Paddy's Hotel (which was called Moby Dick's for most of the '80s and '90s) has been converted into an Eastern European electro-fun pub called Albino's.

Whiter Shade of Whale
There's a nasty-tasting lake in the country of Mexico where the fish walk around on little legs. They are called Axolotl and are prone to albinism. Their bodies are long and ghostly white while their lungs stick out of their heads like bloody red feathers. Due to something chemical lacking in the lake they never turn into what they're meant to turn into and have learned to fuck and

make babies without ever reaching puberty. They can be horny irresponsible tweenagers forever. Flipper finds this all quite admirable but the fact that they eat their babies and have managed to hang onto their legs creeps us out.

I'm an albino whale and I am not unique in this. My eyes aren't pink like a ferret or a lab rat; they're more of a violet color. I just lack pigment. Flipper taught me a great comeback (Dolphin wit and repartee!) if anyone bugs me about this: "You may have the deeper ink hole but I have the biggest pen." I haven't had a chance to use it on anyone yet. Like any other whale I'm a just a giant floating warehouse packed to the lungs with blubber and oil and waxy aromatic ambergris but no jolly whalin' lad's ever going to hunt me down for my melanin.

Apparently my albinism symbolizes different things to different people who in turn project their lurid obsessions on the blank white screen of my hide. My parents' hides were a sort of blue-gray color but there was never any question as to my paternity. Aside from the Captain, the paleness just hasn't been a problem, although I understand how it might be tougher in less tolerant social situations. Down in the deep where the sunlight dims we don't see color anyway. In the Gulf by Galveston you can't see a bloody thing; it's like swimming in a bouillabaisse. Things just bump into you and slide over your tail and fins anonymously. In the clear crystal shallows by the reef everybody's dazzling and gorgeous and while we're happy to eat each other without compunction, nobody thinks they're better than anyone else because of their skin color. That would be stupid.

Flipper says casting an albino as the villain in a book or a movie has become a total cliché. She gives various examples that mean nothing to me, adding enigmatically, "That Da Vinci Cod was a stinking load of wallop." She's my little mine of information.

No Return to the Deep
Here as I lie on the muddy tidal banks of the Severn estuary I can see two great bridges spanning the divide just up the river.

The hippies keep trying to push me into deeper water, back into the safety of myth and mystery, but I'm not co-operating. They have ropes and long pointy prodding tools and pathetic little rubber boats that I could pop like puffer fish if I had half a mind. But I don't need to do anything to resist their efforts; I'm well and truly stuck.

So near but yet so far. I am half in this world, half in that and I'm completely washed up. Curiosity got the better of me too, but after all the good and the bad, the fast and the loose, the damp and the dry (not to mention several hundred pages of dense black and white), who could really blame me? Well that's obvious isn't it? It seems like he always had it for me.

I Prefer Captain Morgan

He was never my favorite sea captain anyway. I prefer Captain Morgan. We used to come across these fantastic little pictures of him stuck to bottles. He stands there smirking evilly with his barrel and his sword all dressed up in red and gold. I love his lacy white cuffs and frilly neck scarf. That's a real sea captain. The bottles we found were down at the bottom of this lovely warm lagoon over by the reef. It was quite a squeeze for us to get in there. They nestled in the soft white sand gleaming and glinting like treasure. They'd probably fallen from some roaring pleasure craft (the ones that nick my fins and hide with their puny propellers) or been thrown from this place Flipper knew called the sundeck of Cap'n A's Crab Shack.

One day, far out in open water I saw a bottle of Captain Morgan spiced rum floating on the surface. It had a piece of paper inside. Flipper said it must have been a message, a message in a bottle. I wondered what it might have said, but I had no hands to get the top off and no way to read it even if I'd grasped the whole concept. I still wonder who it was from and imagine what it said.

Flipper says Captain Morgan was a very bad man, a monster perhaps. Not just a guy on a billboard designed to sell you some spiced-up fantasy lifestyle but a real pirate who did terrible bloodthirsty things and totally got away with it. "All the other pirate people got hung up," Flipper confided. "But Morgan went straight-legit, built a state-of-the-home in a new port and spawned a dynasty. A long tall home for his monster family." And where might that be? "Far over the second big ocean, in the land of the Whales," she replied. We have our own country? Why didn't you tell me before? "Sorry, Ski-slope, I diddle know you were from anywhere at all."

Tell me, Dolphin, is it only monsters that live there?

Here Be Monsters
It's cool to be cast as the anti-hero but I'm not really a vengeful monster. I can't see anything of myself in that depiction at all. All the weird, biblical, supernatural crap was just the Captain, right? I told Flipper about my doubts. "Look, if that all had really happened you'd think some of it would have stuck in my mind?" "Ahem, it may not be your mind it got stuck in," clicked Flipper with some amusement. She'd been reading the book to me for over a month and we'd barely got to New Bedford. "Oh ye of lethal faith! You need some evidence is it? I'll get you solid proof and about time, too," she whelped, swimming off down the length of my gnarly white haunches. I cranked my deep-set eyeball round to see where she was going but she soon disappeared under my tail.

After about five minutes I felt a strange tickling sensation very far away that made me want to breach but within a few seconds it was gone and when Flipper appeared again she was gripping a rusty harpoon between the multitudes of her tiny sharp teeth. It was attached to about six or seven feet of rotten, tangled rope that had clearly been severed with violent force. "This sharpie old thing must have been stuck in your butt ending for somewhat over 160 years," she smirked, slapping her fins together soundlessly. "Are we having a Lion's Den moment yet?" I told her I couldn't handle any more biblical references right now.

All along Flipper had been completely convinced of my true identity and had explored the cracks and furrows of my chalky vastness with diligence and admirable sensitivity until she found the object of her search protruding from my aft regions. "Looky here, Snowball," she said, gesticulating with her snout. "It says in little brass letters: Property of the Pequod. That's the right one then, isn't it?" Proof enough I suppose, except I can't read. I mean, it could have said Welcome to Jamaica Please Drive Carefully for all I know.

There are plenty of real monsters out there in the heaving dark oceans of this world. You don't circumnavigate the globe at enormous depths for hundreds of years without running into a whole gallery of complete bastards.

Take the Hagfish for starters? It likes to bore its way up your back passage and eat you from the inside out, choicest organs first. The only beast ever with a skull but no spine, it swarms in frenzied packs and squirts out a viscous silicate paste from glandular nodules all up and down its ugly phallic shaft that thickens alarmingly on contact with water and chokes anything that attempts to prey on it. Then it ties itself in a disgusting knot which it proceeds to run lasciviously down its entire length to clean off. It has teeth on its tongue and palette and no sense of humor or poetry. It hasn't evolved for hundreds of millions of years. It hasn't needed to; it's a perfect monster.

I bet you've never even seen a colossal squid either? Let alone wrestled one for three days under fifteen fathoms of freezing salt water. Try to imagine thirty-foot-long writhing tentacles that don't just throttle you with sucker cups the size of toilet plungers but hack into your flesh with vicious swiveling hooks that can pivot 360 degrees for maximum ripping and gripping. Then there's the flat dead eyes (as big as basketballs) that stare you down all blank and cold while the monster tries to squeeze your guts right out of your blow holes. They're tough, but if you weren't meant to eat them, why do they taste so good!

I'm big and old and white and ugly but I'm not a monster. And I won't be your scapegoat or your bogeyman anymore either. I know how much you need monsters to sustain all your bullshit dry earth schemes but I wish you'd just leave me out of it, okay? Watch out, I'm going to blow!

The Nova Scotia Tar Baby
There was an old white school teacher in the land of Whales and his boys all called him Sammy. His real name was Arthur Langford. He was stern and reserved and certainly the only person in that school who could remember exactly where this nickname came from. He was named for Sammy Langford, the greatest heavyweight boxer who never won a title.

Nova Scotia looks like a big cannon dangling off the underside of America's eastern seaboard aimed ominously back at New England. Flipper read that in a book called *Halifax, Warden of the North* that had fallen from a manatee viewing platform near the Cape Canaveral launch site. She's a very smart dolphin but you'd think her areas of scholarly expertise would be a bit patchy to say the least, governed as they are by random acts of gravity. They're not patchy; she knows everything!

I don't know how she found out about Sam E. Langford but she did. He had two horrible ring names. First he was The Nova Scotia Tar Baby and then years later The Boston Tar Baby. His skin was as black as mine is white and while Flipper says it's okay for her to call me Chalk-ball or Iceberg or Milky Bar Kid, Sam probably wouldn't have cared too much for the names he got stuck with.

Sam E. Langford toured the world. Once he posed in front of the Eiffel Tower with a silver-tipped cane and monocle. Living the life with the Dixie Kid; he was pimped up pugilist royalty. You called him a monster. The great white hopes wouldn't fight him and even the first black champ, Jack Johnson, refused to give the shorter, tougher man a shot at his title after their prior scrap in 1906. So he pursued Johnson across the country waiting for his chance just as later, when he was old and blind (in your insular city of the Manhattoes), he'd follow younger boxers around the ring by sound and smell, patiently absorbing the body blows, his long arms and bandaged knuckles feeling for the moment to strike.

There are a lot of black people in Nova Scotia. Flipper says they all talk like jolly whalin' lads in '50s movies. They were Africans who got abducted by aliens and dragged halfway across the world to Jamaica. They escaped into the hills and lived free for fifty years. They were called the Maroons. But they were hunted down by the white governor's army and shipped up into the frozen north as punishment.

"You know what the Captain on the spicy rum bottle did after all the pirate mayhem?" asked Flipper. I don't know, more mayhem? "Exactly, your whiteness. King Charlie Stuart made him Guv'nor of Jamaica, the sugar slave island. There's white sugar, brown sugar, and people dying in the fields. Langford name and Morgan name are from the same place and that's how Sammy got his. Sammy gets the white slaver's name and the quiet white teacher gets the black Maroon fighter's name and round and round and back and forth it goes in and out of the Land of Whales."

Is that where Whales go to retire?

Hunted
I hunt and I'm hunted but I never got taken up topside. I've got nicks in my fins from orca teeth, a squid-scarred barnacled back full of harpoons, and I'm happy to crunch the odd whaling boat betwixt my jaws if needs be. I'm a mammal (airy and hairy) so I have to breach once in a while, but when necessary I can hold my breath for hours. There was no boat strong enough, no net big enough to get me up there.

Flipper told me how she got abducted by aliens a long time ago as well. "They caught me up in a net with a load of loose fish. Took me in the dry and give me the fin ring. Said I'm always on their radar from here on inwards; under, over, and through. Knowing every last thing, always."

On the Nature of Hiraeth
Far away a voice is calling, bells of memory chime, come home again, come home again, it calls through the oceans of time.

The silt-choked waters of the Severn estuary lie brown and flat for miles around me. They lap weakly at my vastness. But above the steep fossil cliffs I see the pleasant blue whale-shaped hills of Gwent tumbling off over the horizon, keeping their welcome and waiting patiently to kiss away two hundred years of hiracth.

Whales, whales, bloody great fishes are whales!

The lilting cadences of a fifty-piece whale voice choir drift down from the valleys, through clouds and rain, resonating up (in delightful four-part harmony) from the deep tunnels and shafts you yourselves cut through black earth, rock, and ancient layers of dry bone sediment, from the hillsides with the little crosses where you choked your children on slag so the orange lamps can light the night. Dead families from ancient oceans are calling me.

We'll kiss away each hour of hiraeth...

I'm huge and white and I'm burning up. I'm like a fat bloke sunbathing with his shirt off on a bank holiday Monday. Yes, finally, I'm a beached whale, or what did Flipper call me that one time in the Florida Strait: a bleached whale?

Can I just say I'm bloody sick of you lot standing round staring at me with your cameras and lights and your funny furry microphones (what sort of thieving dinosaur-egg-sucking mammal did you make that from anyway?). This tide sucks but I'm not budging. You can all see that I've lived too long and now it's almost done. Just make sure you smile when you call me a mythical monster.

When you come home again...

Hiraeth is a word that has no direction translation in English (or Dolphin) but we whales understand it perfectly. How could we not; it's our sextant, our compass, our GPS and just one more reason I'm stuck here helpless in these shifting shallows. So what does hiraeth mean again? It implies a longing, a yearning, a primitive and almost sexual ache for home and yes, I was almost there.

Flipper R.I.P.
Whale meat again, don't know where don't know when . . .
She never really recovered from the loss of her library. I mean that metaphorically; it would be insane for a marine mammal to keep a huge pile of books underwater. They'd go all mulchy and the sea worms would have a feast. The little coral grotto of alphabetized shelving I picture was in her head and when it finally evaporated she was devastated. I could tell her sonar wasn't working anymore. Her navigational skills became nonexistent and when she said she could take me to the Land of Whales, I got a sinking feeling in my blowholes. We hadn't been on a trip like that since 1954.

She was a total spy-hopper; always poking her head above the surface to look around. The other Dolphins couldn't care less about your dry land; they're still mad at the insects. But Flipper, as you know, was always obsessed with facts and figures and gathering information. She seemed to suck it in through the airwaves. But in the end it was two-way traffic.

Flipper saw my whiteness as proof of moral purity. She was also convinced I was a virgin. "Hey, Coke-spoon, you never have a nice mating in a long while? You should find a big girl like Pearl!" she clicked with glee back in Scammon's lagoon. Who the hell is Pearl? I enquired. "Mr. Crabs's baby. I saw her in my head, remember? She'll give you some playful rubbing to stimulate your hormones and no worries!" Too much information . . .

Toward the end of our last long journey I was munching a mud hole by the edge of the European continental shelf and

when I looked around she was gone. I peered deep into the abyss
but I never saw her again.

Twenty Questions
What or who am I? Am I alive or dead? Am I fictional? Did I
have my own TV show in the sixties? No, I'm not Tom Jones,
(or Flipper). I'm not a creature, I'm a concept. Am I bigger than
a loaf of white sliced bread? No, I'm not Aer Lingus! Do you
know me? That's a tough question because you think you know
everything. No, I'm not the whale that swallowed Jonah. We're
not even related. Bloody biblical hitchhiker, spat out on some
faraway beach, he should have been grateful. And for your information there is no God and very soon there won't be any mysteries. That's another No! Am I turbulence? Like when you're
cocooned in some tiny commuter jet thousands of feet over West
Texas being buffeted violently by pockets of warm wet air and I
give you a little glimpse of the horror and scale of it all but you
just slide your nose into some magazine from the seat pocket
in front of you and ignore me? Am I a big white cloud? You're
getting warmer. Am I garden gnome syndrome? Am I holding
back the chaos beyond the edge of your vision while the earth
coughs and sneezes in ever more desperate attempts to shake
you off? Can you burn me? Am I a fuel? Yes, you're very warm.
Am I coal? You're burning hot but you'd better shut your bloody
mouths when you're talking to me! Is that a heron? My hump is
huge, my brow is wrinkled. I am quite alone. Do you smell land
where there is no land? Who painted the signposts green? Was
I confused? Did I misread the information provided? How do I
get to the country of Whales?

Message in a Bottle
Ahab's crew watched and waited for the chick inside him to
hatch, like he was a big egg, a big dinosaur's egg. Wait 'til you
cut me open tomorrow and read the messages I've been carrying
inside me and see the broken beaks and armor of monstrous new

predators you have never imagined littered through the tunnels of my gut. You'll never know the half of it.

The Death of Moby Dick
In one early version of the book I am the only survivor. The bit about Ishmael and the savage's coffin got lost at the printers and, despite the first-person narrative, I am the only one who doesn't die. Imagine that! Now you can write a song about me and call it "The Death of Moby Dick" and though the hunt is over and the monsters have finally won, it'll be the last thing to ever cross your lips because now I'm just like you. There's really no difference at all.

Where ever you wander
Where ever you'll be
Up there in the Rhondda
Down here by the sea
We're calling you home, calling you home
And this time it's to stay
And I, I can fly
Over the clouds and over the rain
And I see the greedy hand
Of the vandals who ravaged the land

It's just waiting to happen
The equation's the same
And the rules are as dirty
Though everything's changed
I see it all, you're still so small
And disasters will take new names

And I, I can fly
Over the valleys and over the hills
And I see the secrets, the kisses and quiet

I see the moonlight in the valley
It's taking me back where the earth is still black
And the murderer lies under your feet
It's taking me back

A Sign From God

★

BY DAVID OLNEY

In the year of our Lord 1928, Thomas Braswell was a third year
student at Knox Bible College, located in Morris, Tennessee, a
small town near Knoxville. He was the son of a preacher and
had grown up nearby, in Webb, a tiny farming community of
about three hundred. His father, Asa Braswell, ministered to a
congregation numbering about fifty hardworking rural folk. For
as long as Thomas could remember, he had accompanied his
father and assisted when needed, in the work of God. Births,
baptisms, deaths, and funerals were the commonplaces of his
upbringing. Prayer was as natural to him as conversation with a
family member. Nell Braswell was a loving and dutiful mother
and wife, but it was her husband who gave shape and direction to
the family. Asa Braswell was not a harsh man. He was quiet and
thoughtful. But through some secret power of his personality,
his will was ever law.

And so Thomas grew to early manhood. Having no brother
or sister, he had no rival for his parents' affection or interest. He
was not spoiled, but from early on he was treated as an adult and
participated in the family decisions. At least he participated in
the family discussions. His father, of course, made the final de-

cisions. When he was seventeen he enrolled at the nearby Knox Bible College in preparation for following in his father's, and his grandfather's, footsteps. He would become a preacher. It was never in doubt.

Knox Bible College had a faculty of sixteen good and upright men who refined the faith of the two hundred or so male students and taught them the basics of being a Baptist minister of God. Thomas's whole life had led him in this place and time. It was not so much that he was learning new concepts, as it was that he was learning the proper way to express what he already knew.

But in his third year at the school, the Serpent entered into the Garden of Eden that was Thomas's soul. He could not pinpoint a particular moment when it began, but, little by little, the worm of doubt caused him to question what he had never questioned before. Thomas's doubts could not be said to have arisen, as with so many young men through the ages, with an introduction to those two ancient stalwarts of sin, alcohol and sex. He had no fondness for drink. He had seen, among his father's flock, more than a few unfortunate cases who had destroyed themselves with the locally produced rotgut. And as for sex, he was yet a virgin. While he had the normal urges of a young man his age, he had the good sense not to become a slave to those urges. He believed that sex was a matter for husband and wife. He would wait until he was married to enter that world.

No, his doubts went deeper than the body. He had begun to reassess the very basis of his universe. He never questioned the existence of God, but rather the nature of God. He began to doubt God's goodness. In the intellectual centers of the world, this very question had been debated for centuries. But now such doubts barely raised an eyebrow. They certainly no longer caused burnings at the stake or torture in the secret recesses of cathedrals. But this was not Thomas's world. And he was caught completely unprepared. What brought these doubts on? Certainly, science and technology of recent years had made giant strides.

The ideas of Darwin had crept into even the most isolated areas of the world. Movies, radios, telephones, automobiles, and all the other wonders of this new age had made it increasingly difficult to adhere to the old maxims and beliefs. The roar of the twenties was heard even in Thomas's small acre of the universe.

Doubt turned to mistrust. Uncertainty grew to confusion. Guilt and anger filled the vacuum left by his loss of faith. For that is what it was: a loss of faith. Faith in the all-encompassing love of a benign being, the surety that God knows us even by our names, that His eye is on the sparrow, and that He directs and orchestrates the most minute workings of life everywhere. Given the suffering, the malignity, the uncaringness of the world, Thomas wondered how this could be. Even his own son, Jesus, could not rouse God from his monumental indifference. In another person, this inner struggle would have led perhaps to agnosticism, or even a robust atheism. But Thomas could not make that leap. God must exist. The only question was, was He good or evil?

The battle raged inside Thomas all that school year. As the season turned, and fall grew to winter, he burned with the struggle. He neglected his studies, no longer bothering to go to class. He lost weight. His face grew drawn and tense. He had never been an overly social person but he had had friends at the school. Now he stayed away from human company, choosing to keep his torment to himself. The winter darkness that swallowed the mountains seemed to originate from within his own soul. When spring came to the mountains, it brought no resolution to his crisis. On the contrary, he lost hope.

One day in April, as the dogwoods began to bloom, Thomas went into town and bought a shotgun and some shells. Guns were not unknown to Thomas, having grown up in a community where firearms were a necessary part of farm life. He made the transaction dispassionately. He offered no explanation. Later, the shop owner could recall nothing unusual about his demeanor, nothing strange about his speech. He was simply a young man buying a gun.

Thomas then began walking out of town on the Black Creek Road. He carried the gun, still wrapped in brown paper and tied with a string, in his right hand. The shells were in his coat pocket. It was early afternoon and the sky was filled with rushing clouds borne on the chilly spring wind. He covered four miles at an even, unrushed pace. Although he could not have said exactly where he was going, he had the look of someone somehow guided. Abruptly he turned into the woods. The smell of pine immediately engulfed him. Nature, living and dying, rotting and being reborn, surrounded him in a way he was completely unconscious of. In a clearing in the forest he stopped and looked about. He was encircled by pines and oaks and shrubs. The floor of the clearing was of moss and dried leaves and pine needles. A few birds could be heard and the occasional rustle of undergrowth as some critter scurried by on its appointed rounds. But the overall effect was of deep silence. Thomas unwrapped the shotgun and leaned it against a nearby tree. He moved deliberately, without hesitation. He strode to the center of the clearing where he knelt down on his knees. And he prayed. Sometimes he prayed out loud. More often the words were only in his head. Thomas was unaware of when he was speaking with his voice and when his words were only in his troubled mind. His concentration was so deep that time was rendered meaningless. Seconds could have been hours, and hours, days.

"Dear Father," he prayed, "I come to you in turmoil and confusion, in sorrow and in pain. I acknowledge my weakness and sinfulness. I humbly beg your guidance in my hour of need. I am lost. I am without hope. Father, please show me the way. What must I do to end this torment? In Christ's name I beseech you. Hear my prayer."

Silence.

Again he prayed. Acknowledging his weakness, he humbled himself before an immense and awesome presence. He was willing to shoulder the burden for his sins, to accept any punishment, if only there were some sign, some indication, that his words were somehow heard.

Silence.

Thomas remained kneeling, as if hypnotized, for many minutes. The sun was still shining but now lower in the sky. Its light dappled the trees and danced on the forest floor. He began praying again, more desperately. "Father, I am in need. I have nowhere to turn. There is only darkness around me and only you can bring me to the light. Do not forsake me. I beg you."

Silence.

He remained on his knees. He waited. He did not know how long. Then he spoke aloud, in a dead and ruined voice.

"If you do not make your will known to me now, I will kill the next person who comes down Black Creek Road. Man, woman, or child."

Silence.

"Your will be done," he muttered, and rose to his feet. He reached in his coat pocket and got the shells. He walked to where the gun lay against the tree. He picked it up and loaded it. Then he made his way back the way he had come. He sat down on a rock by the side of the Black Creek Road and waited. The sun was just disappearing behind the western ridge.

Katie McDowell walked with her ten-year-old daughter, Crystal, along the tree-lined street that led them to Ferguson's boardinghouse where they lived in a room just large enough to accommodate two beds, two chairs, a sink, and a small closet. The bath and toilet were down the hall, shared by six or seven other borders, depending on whether a man named James was able to get along with his wife who left periodically for mysterious reasons. There were just the two of them. Hank McDowell, father and husband, had abandoned them three years ago. A veteran of the Great War, he had been wounded at Bellow Woods. The recovery included a considerable amount of morphine, from which he was never able to completely wean himself. He had tried, but the responsibilities of home life, and especially of father-hood, proved too much for him. He lapsed into addiction and one night simply disappeared. Katie's teaching position barely paid the rent, so she helped with the cleaning and the cooking at Ferguson's during the months when there was no school. She was handy at sewing and took the odd mending job, also. It had been a difficult adjustment when Hank left but Katie knew in her heart that his leaving was for the best. Still, she wished that Crystal could have a father. For all that, Katie and Crystal were content with their lives.

By the end of each day, Katie was usually too tired to feel any pangs of longing for male companionship. One day, maybe, but for now she needed to concentrate on the task at hand, which was raising Crystal. Occasionally, the precariousness of their lives struck fear in Katie. Most often, it was only a vague anxi-ety. But a few months before, as Katie and Crystal were walk-ing home, Katie had been aware of a strange old man watching them. It was the mad recluse from the hills who came to town every few months. Some folks said he was a moonshiner. He had watched them with a kind of ferocity that had truly frightened Katie. Then he disappeared and she had not seen him since. She felt a bit foolish for having been frightened. Particularly now, when spring was bringing the earth to life again and hope came with every breath of crisp mountain air.

Katie and Crystal had started attending the Baptist church in town after Hank left. For Katie it was mostly for the warmth of other humans. She had no definitive conception of God. She found Jesus to be a comfort but not in a palpable, here and now sort of way. And that was fine for Katie. Raising Crystal, her work at school, and even the little dramas of the boarding house, kept Katie busy and connected to life. There simply was not enough time for deep religious thought. The workings of God, if, indeed, there was a God, were beyond her understanding. She accepted that. In the meantime, there was work to be done and life to be lived.

Bat Crowell was no good. He knew it. Most everybody who had spent more than three minutes with him knew it. His father, who had abandoned him when Bat was born, knew it. Even his mother knew it, though, of course, it took her longer to face the truth. But when she did know it, she, too, abandoned him by leaping into Black Creek on a bitterly cold February night. Bat was fourteen years old at the time.

But even at that tender age, he knew all he needed to know to survive. He had a roof over his head; the family cabin was so far from town and away from anything that could be termed a path, much less a road, that he was assured of never being bothered by any authority associated with civilized society. And from his mother's Uncle Caleb, who lived even farther back into the woods and higher up in the hills, he had learned the art of moonshine making. Soon after Bat's mother died, her Uncle Caleb disappeared. Bat took over his still. He sold his 'shine to interested townsfolk, doing a particularly brisk business during square dances and revivals. He was by no means a rich man. But he made enough to survive.

His isolation from fellow humans had developed in him an atavistic sense of time. Bat did not know what year, month, or day it was. He could not tell you how old he was. He was unaware of the great events of the world, so he had no reference points to mark his temporal path. But he knew the woods and he knew nature. He could read the wind, or the moss on the trees, and all the secrets of our deep past, forgotten by the modern world. He did not choose his life, but with his ferocious survival instinct, he had learned to embrace it. Forty years of daily sampling of the foul and poisonous concoction he distilled, coupled with the lonely circumstances of his life, had driven him, by any civilized standard, mad. But a feral cunning remained.

He also had his appetites. In fact, that was all he had. On his last trip to town he had walked by the small one-room school. He had seen the prettiest little girl. He stopped, ever so briefly, to admire her. In secret he watched the school waiting to see more of her, to discover the patterns of her life and discern when she was most vulnerable. Later that afternoon, he saw the girl leave, walking hand-in-hand with the school teacher, a woman of about thirty. At a safe distance he followed them. It was clear that the girl and the woman were daughter and mother. Bat understood that the mother would protect her child to the death. She would have to be dealt with. But that would have to wait. Bat went about his business.

The image of the girl burned in his mind, always with him. Stalking through the woods, working at the still, or laying on the cot in his cabin, Bat thought of her. Mother, father, sister, brother, husband, wife, all human relations were somehow foreign to Bat. He had a biological impulse that gnawed at him, demanded that he take some action to satisfy it. Thought had little or nothing to do with it. Companionship? No. Unless ownership is a form of companionship. Sexual desire? Certainly. Insanity? Only in the eyes of townsfolk. To Bat, there was no such thing.

Through the dark winter, Bat brooded on the young girl. Sitting by the fire and sipping away at his jug of moonshine, he stared into the flames and saw her there, innocent and entrancing. The days slipped by unnoticed. Most of the time he did not distinguish the nights from the days, or sleep from wakefulness. When he dreamed, he dreamed he was sitting by the fire thinking on the girl.

Finally the spring came. The earth thawed and the trees began to bud. And Bat stirred from his drunken reverie. As if pulled by an unseen hand, he lurched from his cot and got himself ready to go to town. He thrust a pistol into his belt. He knew he would have to kill the mother. Then he would grab the daughter and bring her out here and they would make a life together.

That was the extent of his planning. He threw a jacket on, put a pint of his homemade liquor in the pocket, and reeled out the door. His eyes were fierce and implacable. It was two miles to the road and another five to town. The sun was going down.

Far above Thomas Braswell, an eagle circled in the sky. The sun, invisible to Thomas, still shone on the bird. It flew in the last moments of the day, delighting in the sun's warmth. Thomas, already wrapped in the shadows, waited.

Bat Crowell walked unsteadily down Black Creek Road on his mission. The evening was falling fast. Soon it would be difficult for a normal human to make his way in the growing darkness. It did not bother Bat. He had traveled this road so many times it was no longer necessary for him to actually see where he was going. He mumbled to himself, like some evil wizard from the distant past, incantations in a secret and terrible language.

It was not until he was no more than ten feet away that Bat took notice of the figure of Thomas Braswell standing in front of him pointing a shotgun. He stopped and stared uncomprehendingly. He did not hear the blast of the gun. The slug hit him square in the chest and knocked him backward several steps. Somehow he managed to keep his balance and stay on his feet. He sank to his knees and died in the attitude of a penitent at prayer.

Moments later, another shot from the gun blew out the back of Thomas's skull. He fell face down in the dirt of Black Creek Road.

And that is how they were found the next morning. One body sprawled in the road, the other absurdly on his knees. The sheriff came out and pieced together what had happened as best he could. He recognized Bat Crowell immediately and was not surprised that the old moonshiner had met a violent end. The young man he thought he might have seen some time before around the town. That it was a murder/suicide was obvious. The motive was not. But the Sheriff was a man of philosophical bent. "Man is certainly a strange animal," he thought to himself as he headed back to his office. He would need some help with the bodies.

"Hurry up, Crystal, or we'll be late for school," called Katie Mc-Dowell. Crystal finished buttoning her coat. She grabbed her books and was ready to go. She and her mother made their way out of the boardinghouse and onto the street that led to the little schoolhouse. It was a glorious morning, full of spring and full of hope. Katie could not help but feel she and Crystal were, in some mysterious way, protected. That this day would lead to another and another and another.

Quantum Gravity (1.)

★

BY CYNTHIA HOPKINS

I've been wanting to tell you this story for a long time. And I don't know why I want to tell it to you. I don't know what difference I imagine it will make. I have tried a variety of methods to forget it and move on, including a series of musical-theatrical stagings of performance-art operettas. I've tried to dismantle it into its component parts, and then freeze those parts like I am a Basilisk, and then re-arrange those frozen parts into new and more entertaining formations. But dismantling the truth into its component parts and re-arranging those parts into elaborate lies has only wreaked further havoc on my life, and if the point is ultimately inner peace, I guess an outside observer would be forced to admit that my method hasn't worked. In fact, it's been almost a complete and utter failure. In fact, for example, it has irreparably broken our friendship, yours and mine.

And the story itself I'm trying to tell is the story of another broken friendship, which like ours got broken through the making of something else. Why do we do these things? We make refractions of our lives, in order to repair them perhaps, and those refractions further obliterate and vaporize and wreck our lives. Those refractions suck out the very marrow of our lives, everything—love, sex, money—sucked up and vaporized in a vortex of work, like Venus and Mars and probably the Earth itself will get sucked up into the vortex of the sun, someday, when it dies. (2.)

So here I go, and I hope you read it (in published form; this way you'll never know for certain whether or not it's you I'm talking to) and I hope you will imagine that you are a being bestowed with the agency of forgiveness. But again, again, I'm avoiding the subject. I wonder if you want to know the real story, though—the one I keep avoiding telling. I think it's important somehow; maybe it will help someone somehow. Because I was just a stupid girl, a stupid idiot college kid with a martyr complex and I felt stuck in a lousy relationship. That, and I drank a little too much sometimes.

I was a stupid college kid and I wanted to be an actress, and I was in a play called *Devil Gat the Desert* and it was based on some Biblical story, an actual section of the Bible, telling about a gang rape. This woman, maybe she's adulterous? She does something wrong, anyhow, and her father or maybe even her husband takes her to this house, this cabin in the middle of nowhere, in open unprotected country, and leaves her there and then tells his enemy tribe or maybe even her brothers to go and do what they will with her; she becomes a sacrifice. She gets thrown to the wolves. It's basically a condoned gang rape right there in the Bible.

My best friend Mary, who'd written the play, had been brought up by a traveling evangelical Baptist minister, who had put her to work evangelizing in story and song from the time she could talk; and her mother was suicidally depressed and justified her depression through unnecessary surgeries. And I said to Mary, "How does your mother find doctors willing to give her these unnecessary surgeries?" And Mary said, "She just keeps on going to different doctors until she finds one who'll prescribe surgery for something." When she was a kid, Mary's mother used to beat the shit out of her on a regular basis (just like your mother, right?) and her parents got divorced later, causing her father to lose his ministry, turn in his badge, so to speak. Her father became a car mechanic after that, and burned all his Bibles. Mary went to stay with him after the divorce, and if I remember correctly, forks began spontaneously flying out of the kitchen drawers. Either that, or he suffered from terrible migraines...

So Mary had written this play and it was like a country-western-musical-poetical-theatrical version of the story of the gang rape from the Bible, and I played the gang rape victim. I was the only woman in the play. And I made friends with this real old geezer, a professor of poetry who really looked like a genuine old-timer cowboy with his long white beard, and skinny frame, and cowboy boots, and three-piece suit. Another good friend of mine was in the play with me, and his name was TJ de Foo, like someone making fun of French people. And then TJ and I started having an affair. We had been friends before the play but in the play we were meant to be lovers and some sort of theatrical lust manifested itself, real or imaginary.

I had always known TJ to be an eccentric character; the first time I saw him, he was in drag as his alter ego Sweetie, and Sweetie was doing a poetry slam. TJ made a kind of half-decent drag queen, in spite of the fact that he was really tall and gangly and had a large nose and tiny inset eyes. He did have good dimples, though. And while TJ exuded a barely suppressed yet palpable bitterness, he allowed Sweetie to let loose as a raging bitch. He was one of those drag queens who uses his fake female form as a delivery mechanism for petty meanness. Sweetie was attractive because she possessed an enviable confidence, confidence on display: she strutted up and down any ordinary hallway with such pomp and circumstance as to make the very walls glitter with her reflected radiance. And apparently, that was enough for me: I fell in love with Sweetie.

So I had a crush on Sweetie but I was friends with TJ, who was a lunatic in his own right. He was a graduate student in Classics, but he had grown up dirt poor, in an Irish Catholic household with too many brothers and sisters. His father beat him when he was little, his mother dressed him up as a girl and made fun of him when he cried. He was damaged. So he studied Plato in the original Greek and honed his wit to produce carefully crafted comments intended to make his girlfriends, and sometimes even his friends, cry. He was ultimately a kind of masochist, I mean a sadist, a little of both I guess. Yet he had perfected a kind of self-righteous charm, precariously balanced against the cruel streak that otherwise might have been his undoing. And there was something admirable about his stubborn ambition, for which this cruel streak served as a mighty source of fuel, the cruel streak in turn fueled by the bitterness of his early life: he had overcome this terrible, brutal childhood to join the ranks of intellectuals, yet he never got over the way he'd been short-shrifted as a kid.

This relationship with TJ, which started out as friendship and then became a torrid affair through the alchemy of this gang rape play we were in together, this relationship which probably would have been doomed in any case for so many reasons, was sort of doubly doomed by the fact that TJ was the best friend of my boyfriend at the time, whose name was Noah.

Noah, meanwhile, was a spindly guy who wore integrity like a banner woven of suffering and dignity, which also served as a cloak to protect him from "meaningless work." Like TJ, he considered his primary occupation to be that of a philosopher, so he never had a job, pursued poetry, wore dark turtlenecks, suffered from a deep depression, and lived off of me. He was out of school and jobless and I was in school and had a job; I paid the bills and cooked the meals and did all the cleaning; you do the math. I had tried to break up with Noah months before the play, but he had sobbed and begged me not to leave him, so instead of ending the relationship I obliterated myself with alcohol every night. We'd go hang out at TJ's house getting wasted and talking about forming a theater company like the one I run now, making shows like the shows I make now, and we did make a show called *Critical Time*, which featured pillows all over the floor to make the floor bumpy. And eventually Noah would skulk home and I'd stay and I'd end up sleeping with TJ. Or Sweetie, depending.

So this one night, this affair's been going on for a few weeks. Noah seems to suspect something is up. He doesn't say it out loud, but he hints at it by singing along with Johnny Cash, "I've been flushed from the bathroom of your heart," while searching my face with a desperate, pathetic, needy look. So I know, and he knows, I think, maybe. And I want it to end, that relationship; I'm desperate for some sort of escape route that will absolve me of responsibility for Noah's heartbroken misery. And because he represented an escape route, I'd fallen in love with TJ, in spite of the fact that he was a malicious prick. But the thing is, I really believed I was in love with that douche-bag asshole nitwit of a crackpot lunatic sideshow freak. But I really did love Noah, also, in spite of the fact that living together wasn't working out so well. Ultimately, Noah was a nice guy. But naturally, though I now view TJ as an escape route out of the relationship with Noah, such calculated thoughts were not on my mind at the time.

In fact, most of my energy was directed toward obliterating any such logical thinking through the miracle of alcohol-induced oblivion. And this particular night, I'd had plenty of time to obliterate. I'd gotten home a day early from being out of town, which I viewed as an ideal opportunity for a tryst with the drag queen. So I polished off a bottle of wine on the train home, and then headed straight for the nearest bar to call TJ, so that I could hook up with him before my boyfriend knew I'd gotten home. But when I called the drag queen to tell him I was home early, he informed me that my boyfriend was at his house at that very moment, but that as soon as Noah left the house, he'd come get me. And this was in the days before cell phones, this was the days of payphones. And so I had to quietly sip my drink and then get up the gumption to stick another quarter in and say, "Hey, is he still there?" Several Southern Comforts (interspersed with phone calls) later, the drag queen announced that s/he was leaving the house and would arrive soon on his/her shiny motorcycle to pick me up (which I also, for reasons inaccessible to me now, deemed attractive then).

So there I was, swaying back and forth—the bar behind me, the empty street in front of me, the sidewalk beneath me—obliteration complete. Mission accomplished, thanks to excessive quantities of alcohol: a bottle of Chardonnay on the train, several Southern Comforts at the bar, and a few beers thrown in for good measure. There I was, reeling on the sidewalk from side to side, swaying in the calm lulling waves of heavenly drunkenness and the power, the heat, the blissful surges of absolute certainty, of enlightenment, lapping at the shores of my consciousness.

I don't have much idea of how long I'd been standing, or reeling, there. I've lost the part in between the barstool and the sidewalk, and there's another black hole (3.) between the sidewalk and the car. But I think the car was an old beat-up brown Cadillac Town Car or black Oldsmobile something. The car pulled up and a man leaned out the window and offered me a ride, I suppose. Leather seats, anyway, and I do remember kissing someone in the car. I don't know if he was in the front or the back seat. There were two men. And I remember drinking something in the car, and the drink spilling into my lap, which is maybe how they got me upstairs? "Change your pants?" And I remember following the two men under fluorescent lighting like a motel entrance, low-income housing complex, through a doorway with glass paneling and up a stairway and down a hallway with wall-to-wall carpeting, dark blue, and into an apartment.

There was a bed in the room, blank walls, like a motel room, empty of decoration, wall-to-wall carpeting, beige, nondescript walls. Dark bedspread. Fluorescent lighting, and a kind of a kitchenette back there toward the right, the second man lurking there, darkening that doorway slightly.

So there it is. I got drunk. I drank too much. I was a blackout drinker (4.). I don't remember most of it. I told you the basics already; you got it out of me rather quickly as I recall. I was strangled almost to death by these guys. This one guy but there were two guys there. They were strangers who wanted my money and I think he tried to rape me, or else he was angry because there wasn't enough money, probably just angry, he certainly could have raped me and I wouldn't have known the damn difference but they did a test at the hospital the next day and it came up "no rape."

And there is a black hole between walking up the stairs and being held down on the bed with his hands around my throat, squeezing, as if to strangle and kill me and I could barely breathe and tried to wrench his hands away. In retrospect, I realize in that moment that he is indeed trying to kill me—but did I realize it then? So much of my brain was shut down that I was operating on pure survival instinct, which in a way may have saved my life, the same mental retardation that put me in the situation probably got me out, the total lack of fear that caused me to struggle against entropy (5.) with all the strength I could muster, standing, lurching up, and screaming as loudly as I could scream bloody murder. And I do remember the two men screaming back. They were manic, they were high on meth or crack and needed money to buy more. I had maybe $60 in cash in my bag which they took, plus all my credit cards, but they wanted more.

There's another gap and I'm lurching out onto a dark road, through a parking lot of some sort of housing complex, toward a payphone under a dim streetlight, the extreme difficulty of remaining upright, my sense of balance almost totally gone, my brain's communication with the limbs slowed to a crawl, gravity swifter than perception, propelled hither and thither by momentum of limbs akimbo, like some prehistoric beast lurching for dear life out from the danger of underwater predators toward the unknown dangers of land and air. And onward across the road toward a payphone and the streetlamps glowing, illuminating everything, a soft yellow glow, a beacon.

And so it could be I did kill them, so that's possible sin number...?

Or else they let me go.

And the next thing I remember is swaying at the payphone and trying to read the street signs through the haze of blurred vision and tell the drag queen where I was. And by some miracle he found the streets on a map and found this payphone and with some difficulty I climbed on the back of the cycle and my jeans were still wet from the spilled drink in the car. And we had sex and I don't remember it but I think he told me the next day we had it and once he said it I did remember flashes of some kind of awkward, violent, loud sex, but was that a real memory triggered by his mention of it or was it a memory cobbled together from other similar but different actual memories to fill in a total blank? And I woke up in the morning and looked in the mirror and he lived in that house, that old crumbling house, and my face was bloated, pale, and swollen and almost a sickly yellow, and there were dark circles underneath my eyes. They were kind of ringed by purple bruises, and my eyes were filled with pools of blood (6.) and I gasped in horror at this image because it was like looking at a monster, a scary monster I didn't recognize, and I didn't know how she got there.

   In re-creating this episode after the fact and incorporating it into my mythology, I developed a theory that I had thrown myself to the wolves just like the woman in the Bible got thrown, and punished, a punishment she deserved. Meanwhile Mary also developed her own interpretation of the events, as some sort of bizarre fulfillment of the events in her play, some sort of punishment perhaps for our blasphemy.

And so, of course, my relationship with Noah was destroyed, the affair with TJ was destroyed, all the friendships were destroyed, the theater company was destroyed, I was destroyed. And the weird thing is (though maybe not so hard for you to understand) I didn't quit drinking after that. I went to see an alcohol and drug counselor who showed me a chart of the downward spiral of alcoholism, and I wasn't anywhere near the bottom, where the alcoholic loses all his money and his wife and his children.

So instead of quitting drinking, I started working on an operetta about the strangulation called *Bullseye: A Lamentation of One Sad Night*, which was sort of modeled on the story of the strangulation, but veiled and filtered through so much esoteric, abstract nonsense that no one would ever have any idea what it was actually about. And it was kind of a country-western-musical-theatrical thing with kind of Biblical language, and so when my friend Mary came to see it, she became extremely upset, and she said, "You've stolen my language." And I thought: "It's not your language!" But in a way, it was. In a way, she was right. In a way, my play was the fragments of my experience and her play all mixed together and re-arranged. And that friendship got broken too.

And now, and now? I've lost so many friends I can't keep track. I'm lonely now, I'm older, I'm tired. I need you to be my friend again.

1. Quantum Gravity: The fantasy or goal of science to provide a single theory describing the whole universe, unifying theories of the very small (as in quantum fluctuations, 1a.) and the very large (as in the theory of relativity. 1b.). Both the theory of quantum mechanics (which could be considered a theory of the very small, especially that which cannot be directly detected) and the theory of relativity (which could be considered a theory of very large forces such as gravity, because gravity—though it is the weakest of the four forces at work in the universe—yet affects everything attractively even over extremely large distances) are ultimately theories of the inevitability of mutual influence, or the interdependence of all things.

1a. Quantum Fluctuations: There are forces at work, such as virtual particles, which cannot be detected (except by their undeniable influence, or subatomic charm), in part because these forces are affected by the act of attempting to detect them (observance affects what is observed).

1b. Theory of Relativity: Time is not completely separate from nor independent of space, but is combined with it to form space-time. Space and time are dynamic qualities: when a body moves, or a force acts, it affects the curvature of space and time—and in turn the structure of space-time affects the way in which bodies move and forces act. Space and time not only affect but also are affected by everything that happens in the universe.

2. Our sun is a star, only much closer up; all stars are suns, only much farther away. Like everything in the universe (and most likely, the universe itself, 2a.) stars are mortal: they are born, live, and die. Stars shine during the interval between the initial collapse of their birth by nuclear fire (stars are basically large hydrogen bombs: their shine is emitted by hydrogen atoms crashing together to produce helium) and the final collapse of their death by gravity. All stars are destined to collapse; they shine in middle age because they are in a state of balance between the energy that explodes them (the hydrogen bomb explosion that creates their shine) and the energy that holds them together (gravity, the force impelling their ultimate demise). Mortality is energy: to live, one must be destined to die. Based on the observance of deaths of stars like our sun, we can expect that when our sun dies, its death throes will scorch the Earth and then suck Earth's atmosphere (and probably the Earth itself, along with Venus and Mars) into its terrible vortex.

2a. During the twentieth century it was discovered that all the stars in the universe (and their planets along with them) are moving away from us. It was therefore logically deduced that the universe is expanding, and that therefore—if the film of time were run backward far enough—everything must have once been at a single point of infinite density, from which we are still exploding outward. The proposed explosion which propelled the outward motion we observe is known as the Big Bang. If the universe was born in this way, the logical expectation is for it (like all things, as far as we know, that are born) to die someday.

3. Black Hole: A black hole is an imploded star whose gravity is so powerful it sucks everything—including light—into itself and renders itself invisible, detectable only by its gravitational influence on the rest of the universe. It is surmised that there is a black hole, with a mass of about a hundred thousand times that of our sun, at the center of our Milky Way Galaxy.

4. Alcohol is a depressant that shuts down the brain in stages, starting from the highest-functioning frontal lobe on down through the mid-brain, all the way to the automatic functions. Just as we bear the spine and eyeballs of our ancestral fishes (as well as the lingering nameless anxiety of the tiny creatures left behind by the dinosaurs, hiding in the bushes when the heavens rained down fire, from which we are descended), our brains bear the traces of their evolution in their very form and content. The seat of the automatic functions (lizard-brain) is located at the base, which is the most ancient part; and the highest or most advanced functions of the brain—morality, ethical reasoning, logic, propriety, compassion, restraint, inhibitions—are seated in the frontal lobe, which is the most recent to evolve. In fact, the frontal lobe is not fully formed in babies; the frontal lobe (the first to shut down from alcohol intake) develops after birth; hence, the tendency of toddlers to behave like inebriated adults.

5. The Law of Entropy states that disorder will tend to increase if things are left to themselves. Entropy is one of the "arrows of time" that distinguish the past from the future, telling us in which direction time is moving; the others being psychological (we only remember the past, not the future) and cosmological (the universe is always moving away from us).

6. Subconjunctive Hemorrhage: An internal hemorrhage stemming from the constriction of blood flow between the head and the body during a strangulation, forcing blood back up into the head, the pressure of which pops blood vessels in the eyes and fills the eyes with blood-red pools of blood.

The Holiday Inn Again

★

BY MARY GAUTHIER

Last night we slept at the Holiday Inn again. It's been a long week, and I'm tired and I don't feel like talking to anybody right now. I'm trying to figure out what the hell I'm gonna to do next.

Night before last, Daddy drank a lot of martinis and got nasty and mean. He started calling mama a whore and a slut and accused her of screwing Mr. Grace, who daddy calls the snaggle-toothed bastard. Mr. Grace is the principal of the school where mama works, and he has a couple of crooked teeth in the front. My sister thinks calling Mr. Grace a snaggle-tooth bastard is funny. She always laughs when daddy says it, so he says it a lot because he likes it when she laughs. But nobody laughed when he said it that time. It isn't funny anymore.

Daddy followed mama around the house yelling all kinds of accusations at her. In the beginning of the fights mama talks back under her breath so we won't hear her, but eventually she'll snap and start screaming at him. Once she gets on a roll, even daddy can't get a word in edgewise. Well, night before last she was on a roll. She went on and on, yelling and calling him a no good dirty son of a bitch. Then it got quiet in the living room. Too quiet.

I was lying in bed in my pajamas with my book in my hands when I heard mama's heels clicking louder and louder as they came down the hallway.

I knew we were going to a hotel before she even called my name.

I was trying my best to read and block out the hollering, but of course I couldn't ignore it. It was so damned loud it could wake the dead for twenty miles around us. I was listening with one ear anyway, just in case mama needed me to pull daddy off her or get in between them and make him shut up when she reached her wits' end.

One night a while back I came running out of my room with my boots on and kicked daddy in the shin as hard as I could. He was standing over mama, yelling and cursing at her. She was crying real hard in her bed, trying to hide under the covers. She had pillows over her head trying to block him out, but I could hear her saying over and over again that she was going to kill herself if he didn't leave her alone. Well, I came flying down the hall straight at him and nailed him so hard with my best field goal kick that he started jumping up and down on his good leg.

Then he started in on me.

He screamed that he wished he'd never adopted me. That the biggest mistake he ever made in his life was taking me in. He called me a fat-ass adopted loser. He said no man would ever marry me because I was too damn fat. No one would ever take care of me if he didn't. That wasn't all. He said even my own parents gave me away. I could expect that from people for the rest of my life. He said I was nothing but trouble, an ungrateful little monster, and if he could, he'd take me back to the goddamned orphanage where I'd be someone else's problem and he would have one less ungrateful bitch to deal with.

He'd quit yelling at mama though, and she didn't have to kill herself.

During another one of their really bad fights, my sister said we should tape-record them so we would have evidence. She put her little cassette recorder at the end of the hall and let it roll while they yelled and screamed. She told me she was gonna call the police and give the police the evidence. I think she got this idea from television. She's too dumb to know that television is different from real life.

The last time she called 9-1-1 to report child abuse, the police came to the house, but daddy was real nice to them. They ended up shaking his hand. They left after five minutes of standing outside the front door talking to him. My sister thinks if we'd had evidence the police would have done something. She's only six years old. She doesn't know that nobody gives a damn about evidence collected by children.

Anyway, like I said, even before I heard mama's high heels clicking my way the other night, I could tell what was going to happen next. Sure enough, as mama got about halfway to my room she shouted my name. "Sissy, start packing your clothes immediately and get your sister packed. We're leaving that dirty no good goddamned son of a bitch."

Running off to hotels at night was starting to get to me. I felt my stomach lurch and my throat tighten.

Every time we go to a motel there are so many things to remember, and I keep forgetting something important. I need to remember our school bags with our books, workbooks and homework, pencils and erasers, ruler, writing paper and calculator. Also, our school uniforms: blue shoes, blue socks, plaid skirts, undershirts, and white shirts. We need our toothbrushes, toothpaste, a hairbrush for my sister and a comb for me. We need clean underwear, too. I try to remember everything, but I always leave something behind. This makes mama start crying again after we get to the motel.

Lately, I've found it easier for us to just get dressed for school before we go to the motel. It all depends on whether there is enough time to do it. Sometimes we leave really fast, but other times mama says let's go and we don't leave for hours because mama decides to stay and fight a while longer.

Often, my sister doesn't change the clothes from the day before. She'll just wear them for a couple days straight. Lately she's gotten in the habit of keeping her school clothes on when she goes to bed. I'm not about to do that. The sooner I can get that skirt off and my jeans on, the better for me. But if we are already wearing what we need for the next school day before we go to the motel, we're less likely to forget something important at the house.

We've been going to motels for over a year now when daddy gets drunk and mean. Instead of getting used to it, I am forgetting something new every time. Last time, I forgot my homework on the kitchen table because my sister was sleeping by the time mama finally decided we were leaving. I couldn't get her to wake up enough to pack. I shook her and yelled "Pack" right into her ear, but she just kept going right back to sleep. So I packed for her, and Mama carried her to the car. Trying to remember all of her books and clothes and stuff made me forget my own damn homework on the kitchen table, which I knew was going to get me in trouble in math class the next day.

I tried to make mama turn around and go back and get it, but she wouldn't. She said she'd write a note. Of course she didn't. I got in trouble even though I tried to explain what happened to Mrs. Casper before class started. She made me run all the way to the flag pole and back five times as fast as I could, and by the time I was done I was sweating and breathing hard for a good fifteen minutes. Then she made me put my desk at the front of the room and sit there for an hour facing the whole class. I was so embarrassed that I swore to myself that one day I was going to kill daddy for making this happen to me.

Yep, the fun is over, and I don't want to stay in motels any more. It was kind of fun at first because we had never been to a motel except once on our family vacation to Florida. I was thinking it would be a big adventure like Navarre Beach, and we'd have a great time in the game room and then go to the all-you-can-eat buffet breakfast, but the Baton Rouge Holiday Inn didn't have a game room or a buffet breakfast. They did have an ice machine in the hotel hallway, and my sister liked to push the button and watch the ice pour into the ice bucket. She insisted on filling it up every time we checked in, even if we didn't need ice that night.

Also, when we stayed in a motel mama took us to Dunkin Donuts in the morning on the way to school. When we slept at our house we never ever got to do this, and Dunkin Donuts are a great way to start the day. I love Munchkins, especially the glazed chocolate kind. Mama gets us a big box of assorted Munchkins at the drive-through window. We eat the whole thing in the car before she drops us off under the breezeway at school. My sister and I used fight over who gets the most chocolate ones, so lately mama tells the lady at the drive-through window to make half the box chocolate glazed.

Sometime mama turns the radio on in the car on the way to school, and when "I Will Survive" starts playing, mama turns it up loud and belts out the chorus, tapping her wedding ring against the steering wheel. I hate that damn song. I think it is down-right stupid, but mama loves it and she goes nuts every time it comes on.

To be honest, I don't care so much about the damn donuts anymore either. And the thrill of the ice machine is wearing off for my sister.

We're just sick and tired of running to motels in the middle of the night. I mean, what's the point of packing and going to motels when we go back home the next day on the school bus and walk in the house like nothing even happened? That's one of the hardest parts, knowing we are going to have to turn around and do it all over again the next time daddy gets good and drunk on martinis.

But there's no stopping mama when she decides we're out of there. So night before last I started packing the book bags again, making double sure that I had all my schoolbooks and homework and underwear. I forgot clean underwear once and I'll never do that again. I felt dirty all day the next day at school and I couldn't relax.

I banged on my sister's bedroom door and walked in. She didn't hear me knocking because she was in the very back of her closet with her Sesame Street music up loud, which is what she always does when it gets bad.

I said, "Let's go."

She looked at me like she was gonna start crying, and I said, "Don't be a damn baby." I said. "Pack your books, get your school uniform, let's go."

She said, "Sissy, I don't wanna go."

"Okay then," I said. "Fine. You stay home with daddy. Mama and I are going. You two will have a lot of fun here tonight. He's had about ten martinis and a six-pack of beer and he's still drinking."

Well, the lip quit trembling right then and there. She got mad as hell at me and started throwing her stuff in her bag.

She switches emotions so fast it makes your head spin. She goes from crying to being pissed off in about a half a second, and when she decides to throw a fit she lets loose with everything she's got. She thinks because she wasn't adopted and I was that makes her better than me. I think because she wasn't adopted she's spoiled and babied. She's a brat and she gets away with murder.

One time she grabbed the fireplace poker and chased me around the house after I called her a spoiled rotten brat. I quit running after a while because I was winded. Just stopped on a dime and stood with my arms crossed and stared into her demon eyes.

"What the hell do you think you're gonna do with that poker anyway?" I yelled at her.

Well, she lifted it high and whacked me with it and broke my damn nose. She's got one hell of a temper. But this night, though, she started packing her stuff instead of throwing a tantrum.

After several trips in and out of the house for things we forgot, with daddy yelling and following us in and out and in and out, mama finally locked us into the station wagon and started the motor. Daddy followed us to the end of the driveway. His lips were moving and his hands waving, but we couldn't hear him because our windows were rolled up. He kept banging on the windows and trotted beside the car as mama backed out of the driveway. This scared the hell out of me. I thought we'd roll over him and kill him. But we made it to the street. The last we saw of him that night he was still standing and yelling at the end of the dark driveway. Mama hit the gas hard and we were off to the Holiday Inn.

By the time we got there it was really late, so the next day I could hardly stay awake in class. It's hard to get up when the wake up call comes in at 5:00 a.m.

I played tetherball with Leslie Planters at recess, and she beat the hell out of me every time. Three games straight she kicked my butt. I couldn't even focus on the ball she was hitting it so hard. She had it wrapped all the way around the pole so fast I was left standing there speechless with my hands up in the air. That's what lack of sleep will get you.

Leslie's my best friend. Her parents are divorced and her father lives in an apartment. We go see him sometimes on Saturdays, and Mr. Joe always gives us shiny fifty-cent pieces. Sometimes I grab a few extra. He has coins lying all over his apartment and I am banking on the idea that he won't miss a few.

After I lost at tetherball I was so tired I almost fell asleep in class. I put my head down for a little rest and I was starting to doze when Sister Helen said, "Sissy, can you please tell me what you are doing with your head down on that desk?" She really hates it when kids don't pay attention in her class. I said, "I am sorry, Sister. I will wake up." It was a very, very long day for me.

After school I took my usual bus home. I knew we might end up at the Holiday Inn again, but mama always makes us start out at home. I walked home from the bus stop thinking that it was time for me to do something about this situation. It was looking to me like I was going to have to be the one to save us.

So when I got home I walked into the living room and went straight to the newspaper. It was folded up messy on the stained yellow ottoman next to daddy's chair. An ashtray overflowed with ashes and cigarette butts on the table. It stunk up the whole room. Crumpled empty packs of Kent were lying in the ashes next to empty beer bottles and dirty martini glasses. Some of the cigarette burns on the arms of daddy's yellow leather chair were shiny and new. The coffee table next to the chair had rings on it, where daddy's drinks stained the wood in the shape of a glass. I ignored daddy's mess. I grabbed the classified section of the paper and took it to my room to look at the listings for apartments.

There were several big complexes listed, mostly with one- and two-bedroom apartments, but I figured we needed something bigger. There were only a couple of bigger apartments listed, and every one of the three-bedroom apartments had swimming pools. This was exciting! I am a natural born swimmer, and I have several trophies from placing high in swim meets at the Clubhouse pool to prove it.

We had our own rooms in our house here in Tara subdivision, and I was thinking that we'd certainly need our own rooms when we moved out. Seemed to me we needed a three-bedroom apartment with a pool. After all, I am eleven years old now, and not about to share my room with my little sister. I need my privacy so I can read and listen to the radio in peace.

When mama got home from work I told her what I had decided.

"I circled some apartments in the paper, mama. Let's go looking this weekend when you aren't working. There's one with a swimming pool that sounds great."

Mama frowned. She was terrified of bodies of water, all bodies of water. She never took us to the pool, daddy always did. The pool made her nervous. I knew the pool would be a problem for her, but I figured I'd try for it.

"Okay baby, I'll think about the apartment. But it's not safe for you kids to be around swimming pools."

I figured she'd bend my way on that once she finally saw how nice a pool could be. I have a friend from school with a swimming pool and cabana in her yard, and it's always a lot of fun when I go there. If we could find a place like Ann Goode's and make a new life, without daddy and the horror, maybe things would finally get good for us. There'd be some other families there, too, maybe we could all have cookouts at the pool like we did at Ann's house, eat hamburgers and hot dogs and play pool volleyball.

It would be great!

The apartment idea was growing in my head, and getting me more excited by the minute.

"I'm sick of going to motels. I think we should get an apartment so we don't have to keep packing and unpacking over and over again."

The sun was starting to set outside the kitchen window, and as I glanced out onto the street I felt that sinking feeling that always hits me that time of day. It feels like something strong is gripping the inside of my throat and tightening around it. I knew there wasn't much time left to talk about apartments, because when daddy gets home from work everybody scatters and tries to stay out of the line of fire till dinner is ready.

"Can we go looking tomorrow? Tomorrow's Saturday, you don't have to work, and we can spend the day together finding us a new place to live. Please, mama, please?"

I knew that the "spending the day together" line would get her. I haven't wanted to spend the day with her in a long time. On Saturdays I have her drop me off at the library. I stay there all day reading books in the kids' reading room. Lately, if I am not at the library on Saturday I am with Leslie, visiting her dad.

"You keep saying you are going to leave daddy. You always say we aren't coming back when we leave to go to the motel, but we keep coming back. Why do we keep coming back? Let's get another place to live where we don't have to go to a motel anymore, a place where we can be happy. I don't want to live here with daddy any more!"

I knew that if I started crying I might swing her my way, so I worked up a few big tears, hoping it would get her to agree to a new place with a swimming pool. But she was only looking at me with one eye now. The other eye was looking out the window, watching for daddy's white Buick to pull into the driveway and put an end to this conversation about apartments and swimming pools. I could tell she didn't really want to go looking for a place for us to live, but she was quiet enough for me to feel like I might convince her if I kept trying.

Just when I started crying good and almost had her saying yes, I heard daddy's car turn into the driveway. Mama's face switched from slightly confused to completely frozen. Damn it! I lost her.

Daddy's car door slammed. A couple of seconds later, he walked in the back door. Mama was standing over the sink, looking out of the window onto the street with her face as hard as the chicken in the freezer when he walked in the kitchen.

He walked right up to her and laid a kiss on her cheek.

"Hey, baby," he said, but she didn't move a muscle.

He opened the cabinet and got his gin and vermouth out. He opened the fridge and got out the olives. He pulled some ice cubes from the freezer and smashed them with a big spoon in his hand. Tossed them in his glass, poured in some olive juice, and strained a martini. He took a big sip. "Ahhhh, damn that's good." Then he turned to mama. She was still standing at the window looking out.

"Baby, how was your day today?" he asked her, lighting a cigarette.

He was standing there with that drink and cigarette in his hand acting like last night never happened. She looked at him without changing her expression, then looked away again. Then she turned and walked right past him without saying a word. She headed straight to the bedroom and slammed the door.

He drank the whole martini in one big gulp, made another one, crushed the cigarette in the ashtray, and headed for the bedroom. He sleeps in my sister's room now since a knock-down drag-out fight they had a few years back, and my sister sleeps with mama. But his clothes are still in there, and he keeps his wallet and change on the dresser. He calls it his room even though he doesn't sleep there anymore. He gets really pissed when she locks the door. Well, she locked the damn door.

He started banging on the locked door. "I need to talk to you. Open the goddamned door."

"Leave me alone," she yelled.

"Goddamn it, woman, get out here and cook us some supper. Me and the kids are starving and there's nothing in the refrigerator to eat."

After a little while she came out of the room and went straight to the kitchen. I could hear her slamming cabinet doors and banging pots and pans.

Daddy sat in his yellow chair relaxing with his third martini and a beer, another cigarette, and the paper.

I hadn't said a word since he got home. The minute he walked in from work I took the classified ads to my room and put them in my school bag. I knew how mad it would make him if he knew I was looking for an apartment. He doesn't want us to go to motels to begin with, so I could only imagine what he'd do if he knew I was looking for an apartment.

About a half-hour later mama called us from our rooms to eat, and we all sat down for dinner. No one said a word as mama served us fried eggs, grits, bacon, and biscuits. My father sat staring at his plate as though he couldn't believe what he was seeing.

"Goddamn it," he said. "What is this shit?

"I work all day and come home and get served breakfast for dinner?"

He picked up his plate and threw it hard against the wall. The plate bounced and broke when it hit the floor. Daddy's food smeared all over the wall. A glob of egg yolks and grits stuck to the wallpaper for a second and then began sliding to the floor. The biscuits and bacon ricocheted off the wall and skidded under the dinner table. My sister started crying and ran to her room.

Mama went nuts. She jumped out of her chair, screaming, "You dirty no good dirty son of a bitch, I've had it. You've done it now. I swear to God I am leaving your sorry ass and I am not coming back. I can't take it this shit any more. I am at my wits' end."

I could see where this was headed and it made my throat feel like it was closed up all the way. I could hardly breath my throat was so tight.

"We're leaving," she said

After we checked into the motel, I pulled the classified section of the newspaper out of my schoolbag.

"Mama, let's pick out some apartments to look at," I said.

She sat on the hotel bed with me, and we looked at the apartments I had circled. She didn't say much, but it seemed to me that she might be giving in to my idea.

This morning we went apartment hunting. The name of the apartment complex mama agreed to look at is Sherwood Oaks, and the address is close to our school, off Government Street.

We drove into the parking lot slowly, looking around at the two-story apartments, trying to find the office to meet the lady we talked to on the phone. She said they have two empty units, and we're supposed to meet her at her office. After a little while of circling around the parking lot and not seeing the office, we ended up at the pool and clubhouse, and I get excited.

"Let's get out and go look at the pool!" I said.

Mama parked the car and we all got out. The first thing she said was, "Sissy, hold your sister's hand."

The three of us stood behind the chain-link fence at the edge of the parking lot, looking at the pool and the clubhouse in total silence. I had one hand wrapped around the fence, and one hand wrapped around my sister's hand. Mama stood there with her lips pursed, looking pale and withdrawn.

There were kids playing in the shallow end of the water, laughing and running around and diving in. Some other kids had a beach ball and they were playing water dodge-ball while their mothers sat in lawn chairs in their bathing suits talking to each other and reading books. Someone had a portable radio on, and Stevie Wonder was singing "You Are the Sunshine of My Life."

There was a really good diving board at the deep end of the pool, and some older kids were bouncing high on it and doing flips and fancy dives. A man stood by a grill cooking, and a bunch of little kids sat by the side of the pool, soaking wet in their bathing suits, eating hot dogs the man grilled for them.

Suddenly, mama turned around and looked back at the car. "Let's go," she said.

My sister kept hold of my hand as mama began to walk back to the car. She looked up at me with her eyes wide.

"Do something, Sissy," her eyes said.

She squeezed my hand hard. I felt my heart sink.

"Mama, aren't we going to the office now to meet the lady and look at the apartments?" I called after her.

She stopped for a minute, turned back, and looked past me at the pool.

"No," she said softly.

"No," she said again, this time louder.

"We're leaving. It's just too dangerous to have you kids around water."

BY ZAK SALLY

★

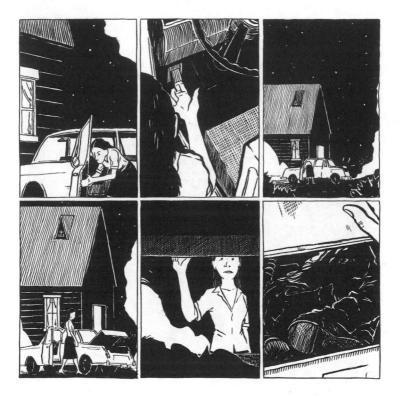

SALLY 02

The Thicket
★
BY RENNIE SPARKS

It was almost dawn when the Reverend Blackwell dragged his wife up to the cliffs of Mount Pleasant. Carrion birds stared down from thorny nests high in the wet crevices.

"Mercy," Rosemary wailed. "Mercy!" as he dragged her along the rocky path. Blackwell did not listen. He ran his blade across her throat in the shadows of the dripping peaks.

"Husband..."

She tried to speak, but her mouth was full of blood. He wiped his knife clean in the dripping bramble then turned and headed back down the mountain. He did not look back. Once, many years ago, Rosemary saw a fox running across a moonlit meadow with a white hare hanging from its jaws. Oh, the contented stare of that hare as it passed, still breathing, in the mouth of its killer. Yet Rosemary felt only rage as Blackwell dragged the knife across her throat.

∗∗∗

She remembered him crying, "I love you! I love you!" as they sat on the shores of Lake Twilight that terrible night when he begged her to marry him. How the grass teemed with crickets.

How they jumped madly up Rosemary's shawl screaming, "Kill it do! Kill it do!" as she beat her fists against Blackwell's chest and struggled to be free of him.

He did not know why she wanted to run from him. He did not know why her eyes were drawn over the cliff edge to the valley where wolves tore at the carcass of a deer. He did not know that she would have preferred to throw herself to those snarling beasts than return his kiss.

The wolves knew. They ran in circles, shaking their muzzles and howling as she stood weeping upon the boulders (some of them even leaping up on two legs as if to get that much closer to her).

Yet she did marry Blackwell. She spoke her vows with a grievous bullet wound in her breast, burning and bandaged beneath her silk wedding dress.

***

There came no thunderbolt. There came no chorus of angels. Blackwell arrived back at the stone pillars of Whitehaven as dawn spread across the town. He went home and polished his boots (the trail had been muddy and her blood had splashed wildly). Still the Lord made no answer.

His heart felt light and strong as he sat in his rocking chair before the fire with only the boy now (asleep upon a goose-feather pallet, not knowing his mother was already dead). Blackwell thought of Rosemary's body growing cold upon the mountaintop and he was glad. It was almost enough to make him forget his shame. How he lay upon her in their straw bed as the insects laughed among the bushes and Rosemary held her body rigid like a piece of wood until he rolled away without finishing the foul act.

How many nights did she lay there mocking him before she (Whore! Harpie! Succubus!) showed him her swollen belly and he knew she had lain in the forest with another man.

He could not forget entirely. No man could be made to forget such things entirely. Could he forget how she gazed into a puddle of water to find where the Governor's men were riding? Could he forget how she plucked the tail feathers from a hen to know if rain should fall or that a blackbird hopping among the briars told her where blueberries ripened?

When they strolled around the millpond, Blackwell heard toads begin to sing at the sight of her. He saw black fish leap into the air as she stood at the muddy shore.

The faint tracks of wolves ran across the dusty slate roof of their cottage. Snakes gathered in such numbers at the bottom of the well that none could bring up a bucket without finding it full of writhing serpents.

A small, dark wart appeared on the underside of her arm and it would not bleed even when pricked with a heated pin. She did not scream nor even stir in her sleep as he cut through it with his knife.

Was it possible to forget any of this?

***

She heard the awful sound as she lay beside her husband and tried to sleep. She covered her ears and rolled from side to side, but the sound would not leave her (that soft pitter-pat upon the roof as if a toad hopped a slow, wet circle above her). She sweated and rolled until her legs were tangled in the woolen blankets and her hair fell loose from her cap in sweating curls.

Yet the noise grew louder: pitter, pat, pitter, pat...Owls beat their wings against the shuttered window and mice scurried across the dirt floor, but still the pitter-pat grew louder (as if now not one, but several toads were hopping a circle upon the roof).

At last she slept. She dreamed she washed great loads of bloodstained sheets in foul-smelling buckets of water. Tall men in golden capes shot cannons at the sea.

"Do you love us, mother?" A tiny chorus of voices asked. "Will you always love us?"

Rosemary looked down and saw that her clothes had fallen away and a little green toad suckled hungrily upon each of her narrow breasts...

In the morning her nightgown was unlaced. There were bite marks upon her flesh and a mark like a dark hand upon her thigh.

She sat on a velvet tuffet in the church green working her embroidery (a linen sheet twined with oak leaves at the border). The summer light fell upon her and birds sang sweetly as she drew her needle through and tried not to see the black ants marching through the grass blades or the dead crickets dragged upon their backs.

Oh, but there fell to her lap a single gossamer thread with a black spider dangling at its end! The spider hung a moment in the air, waving its glistening legs, then dropped to Rosemary's thigh and quickly (so quickly she had no time save to gasp and drop her needle to the grass) raced down the folds of her skirt and into the crevice between her legs.

How she screamed! How she ran! How the great stones broke free from the cliffs above her and came tumbling down upon the church steeple.

***

No, Blackwell did not forget. Not even after he had taken a hammer and pounded Rosemary's bones to dust and rolled the dust within a simple dough and fed this bread to the blackbirds swooping the shadows so that not a trace of her remained upon the Earth! Not even then did he forget.

He fled across the ocean, but even upon the rolling waves, as he lay in his cabin sick with fever, he forgot nothing.

The fever made his heart flutter and it seemed the very blood in his veins had turned to fire. Still he felt her hands upon him, cold as death. He shivered and cried out and a great wind swept him from his fevered flesh, high into the sky. The dark ship spun below him like a leaf on the water, but he looked away and rose toward the light.

There, among the singing angels and the blessed trumpets, he glimpsed the silver wings of the seraphim spinning like great wheels at the very center of the sun.

"Let me die!" He cried to them. "Let all things die!"

Lo! The trumpets rang, the golden clouds shifted, and multitudes of demons fell screaming from the air, their dark wings trailing blood across the sky. And was not Rosemary among those devils, screaming in her flames as she fell, chased for eternity by carrion birds? Yes, she was there, but she was here with him, too. Her naked, sweating skin filled the very air around him and she clawed at his flesh like a dog, her tongue running wetly down his chest.

He heard faraway explosions and saw great cities collapse under gigantic waves. He saw enormous glass towers crushed like eggs and ships that circled the sky dropping fire upon the Earth.

The leaden clouds filled with dead souls. He saw them and rejoiced. He longed for the end of the world! He longed for all things fleshy and warm, hungry and wet, to be banished forever!

Yet how beautiful Rosemary had looked the first night he spied her. His heart sang to see her there in the damp, dark forest...

He was roaming the night woods with torch and gun, a black-haired youth hunting roe deer. There, in his flame, two red eyes reflected. He knelt and aimed true. Only as the shot rang out did he see that it was not a deer, but a young woman in a scarlet cloak fallen before his musket fire.

She had lost her way in the forest and had been many days without food. She was so delirious with hunger that she sang with the nightingales as he carried her, grievously wounded and trailing blood, down to the stone pillars of Whitehaven. Even then, as he carried her down the narrow path and her golden hair trailed in shining rivulets over his arms, even then he longed to throw her down and thrust himself upon her. The very smell of her blood brought a frenzy to his heart and he briefly pressed his lips to her wound.

The foul sin of lust! The foul sin of life! He cried out in his sea fever as he swirled through the clouds (and far below in the ship's cabin his boiling flesh, soulless and mad, screamed and spit and fought to continue its putrid life). How he longed to follow the dead into the bliss of sacred oblivion. If the Lord's voice did not wait then at least His silence would.

Far, far away. Blackwell heard his son whispering as he mopped his father's sweating brow. What a helpless pity overwhelmed Blackwell as he stared down at the boy. The glow of youth was upon the young man's cheeks, but Blackwell saw the maggots within (there, waiting in the skull crevices and the ear canals and the folds of the boy's churning gut) and he wanted only to regain enough strength to take up a hammer to smash his beloved boy's skull to dust. He would smash his own skull, too. He would kill everyone on the ship, even the rats hidden in the crates down in the darkest holds.

***

What terrible thoughts lurked within her! What daydreams Rosemary had of the Governor's white stallion trampling her as she watched the great man trot along the high street in his silk brocaded trousers.

Why could she not be gentle and calm like Mother? The woman had once mended a broken wrist simply by laying her hands upon it. Mother carried rye cakes through the darkest thickets to feed the leper colony at the far side of Mount Pleasant. She invited into her own bed those dying of the rosy plague, spooning duck's broth to their swollen lips until the death rattle began.

Mother had once lured and trapped an evil spirit inside a simple clay jar. A man named Wigworth, a sheep farmer from Whitehaven, was attacked by sprites while inadvertently drawing water from an enchanted well. The poor bedeviled man was soon found raving upon the church green, convinced that the light falling from the stars was interfering with his very thoughts.

Mother took salt and rose thorns and dropped little pinches of each into the earthenware jar, all the while crying, "Be gone! Be gone!" as the night died away. As the last star faded Mother slammed the lid upon the jar and the ailing Mr. Wigworth sat up clear-minded.

Was it so much then to believe that Rosemary could learn to lance boils and quiet coughs, to balance biles and the like? Even Mother admitted that Rosemary had a gift for knowing when trees were to fall, horses to buck, and children's limbs to be crushed under wagon wheels. Of course Mother cruelly (and wrongly!) suggested it was Rosemary's very presence that brought these calamities about. Rosemary did admit that when a house burned down, a dog went mad, or a river overflowed, she was often the first to wander upon the tragic scene.

Once, during her brief days as a student, she was called to recite a poem at the front of the class. As she walked up the row of snickering boys toward the lectern, a chance windstorm sent a great chestnut tree toppling over upon the schoolhouse. The teacher (a white-wigged gentleman named Carver) was killed instantly and several students were trapped for days under heavy black branches teeming with tree toads.

Still, there had always been healers in the family. Rosemary's grandmother was a stooped crone who lived in a cave in the oak forest. She gave blackberries to children in exchange for locks of their hair. Granny Green lived so long in the oak forest she learned the language of sparrows. Alas, it was the sparrows who sang her the recipe for a spider bite tonic that, once administered to the good people of Whitehaven, caused many to dance for days on end. The villagers danced and danced until they collapsed in nervous exhaustion or threw themselves into the raging river to be dashed upon the rocks (anything to end their terrible leaping and prancing). The surviving townspeople covered Granny Green in pitch and feathers and set her ablaze at the crossroads. She burned brightly for a fortnight, screaming so loudly that all were forced to bind their heads with yards of cotton else lose their reason. At last Granny Green's fire died out. Her body turned to a silver ash that darkened the sky to night as it blew away.

Rosemary knew little of Granny Green's mother. It was said she was called the May Queen. One spring evening, when the rains had not come and the young and the old had begun to curl up in their beds like wilted flowers, the May Queen took up a silver dagger and stabbed herself in the heart. Her life's blood fell across a field of dead barley and it, at once, stood firm and began to bloom. Alas, though she saved the town, it was later rumored that the May Queen took a goat to her bed and so the tall wooden statue erected in her honor was taken down and cut to kindling.

***

Five years before the boy was born, late on a summer night, Blackwell traveled alone upon the royal road. He spied an old woman in the moonlight. The crone raised a gnarled fist and bid him tarry. She had only one eye (the other merely a scarred and empty hole). This one-eyed hag carried caged doves to market upon her back and one of her birds had escaped to the treetops. Its wings were cut and it could fly no higher.

Blackwell climbed an oak tree and pulled the dove from the end of a trembling branch with his leather-gloved fist. How mournfully the creature sang as Blackwell thrust it back into the cage and it seemed the other doves joined its heartbroken melody.

The one-eyed hag laughed wildly at the terrible bird song (while he felt his own heart utterly shattered at each peak of its trilling lament).

The hag winked her lone eye at Blackwell and pursed her dried lips as if she meant to invite him into her arms. Instead she offered him a red apple.

He did not hesitate for he was hungry enough to suck river stones. He brought the ripe fruit to his lips and bit into its juicy flesh. Oh, it was sweet! It was so sweet that after only one bite his body shuddered and he whirled about, seeing ghosts in the shadows. He fell dizzily to his knees and the hag stood tall and spoke...

Here be my thanks to thee
Though you wish it may not be
There is just one way to know a witch
Though you doubt it, I insist
As the water boils fair
A lock of your own cut hair
Thrown into the steaming pool
Brings forth the one bewitching you
Though you wish it may not be
A familiar face is what you'll see

He stood and slapped the withered whore to her knees, crying, "How dare thee speak to a man of God so profanely! You shall burn in the Devil's arms!"

The one-eyed hag laughed madly as he cut her down and cried, "Gladly I go to his arms! Gladly I kiss his buttocks! Gladly I take him into my mouth and into my ass!"

He beat her with his boot and cane until she spoke no more and still he beat her until it seemed he shattered her like an egg's shell and there remained nothing of the one-eyed hag or her doves save a pile of dried twigs.

Yet his hand, where he had slapped the hag's face, now burned and swelled. A terrible bile weeped from it that greatly wore him down so that when he returned home he took to his bed for many days.

Two years passed in which each day he became weaker and his hand shriveled further until it could no longer be used (and the other hand, too, began to curl like a drying leaf).

When he did manage to rise from bed he found he was too weak to tie the ribbons at the hem of his breeches, but too ashamed to beg Rosemary's help. Yet, she grew wondrously hale and red-cheeked! She laughed and danced about the house, singing to the very maggots that swarmed his festering wounds!

***

Rosemary dreamed that Mother was alive again. They climbed together to the top of Mount Pleasant in the new-fallen snow. Mother's golden hair glowed in the winter sun and it seemed that even the skin of her face gave off a silver light that spread out across the white valley in rippling streams.

"Mother," Rosemary whispered. "Teach me to heal the world!"

"The world needs no balm," Mother whispered as she brought a handful of snow to her rose-red lips. "Even its cold is as it should be!"

Mother opened her arms and took Rosemary to her breast. How warm Mother's skin! How the snow melted and the grass grew green! Rosemary burned as Mother pulled her in closer (for now the sun shone fiercely above and it seemed the fields were in flames).

Mother screamed and fire roared from her boiling feathers so that Rosemary struggled to pull free. She wanted to run away down the snow-covered hills, but Mother's golden beak opened wide and took Rosemary into its steaming mouth.

"Even its heat," the great burning bird screamed, "is as it should be!"

Mother was long dead now. The Governor's men had ducked her upon the witches' stool until she sank and proved her innocence, but breathed no more. A crowd had gathered at the river's edge, drinking and laughing as Mother tossed in the icy currents. When Mother's corpse was finally pulled from the rippling water with a thatcher's hook twisted in her golden hair, her gray eyes bulged and her mouth oozed a stream of muddy water. How the drunken mob laughed!

Late into the night Rosemary knelt over Mother's corpse as the trees groaned and snapped in the wind. Mother's eyes were darkened to black and they were empty and cold as the very rock her body lay upon. Yet there was something opened in that blank stare: a faraway door opened to the night and the flicker of a tiny candle flame within. Rosemary imagined moths flying into the holes of Mother's empty eyes, drawn to that faint light where her soul had once lived.

Lo! Even as she knelt there praying, a dusty-winged moth landed upon Mother's dead cheek and Rosemary watched as it crawled slowly across Mother's frozen stare.

With a sudden gasp, Mother's dead mouth opened and three black eels came wriggling out from between her blue lips. They flopped and twisted upon the rocks then fell to the river and disappeared.

* * *

Great, black flies gathered about Blackwell's burning hands and upon the spittle that dried across his parched lips. All the while his wife sat singing for hours while he lay upon the bed too weak to call out for a cup of water.

He prayed. He found strength for nothing else. He prayed mightily, alone upon hilltops and surrounded by his brethren within the church. Yet, as ever, the Lord was silent, and he, Blackwell, grew weaker still.

In the third winter he had gathered a great band of followers who knelt at his feet and took all that he spoke as the very voice of God (and so all heard the Lord speak save he who claimed to hear Him!).

Blackwell could no longer walk without canes. His hair fell out and at night he vomited up bloodstained papers with obscene drawings upon them. He vomited up the clawed feet of birds and little parcels of dog hair. He found red worms in his chamber pot and black flies swarmed about him even as he stood before his followers speaking of Heaven (and all were sure it be proof that the Devil was greatly dismayed at his words!).

His wife's belly began to swell.

"But husband," Rosemary cried, laughing merrily at his surprise and alarm. "Do you not remember? Do you not know how you awaken each night like a wild beast and take me so hungrily upon the very dirt floor! Do you not remember how you met me upon the royal road and lay me down upon the moss and the oak trees were full of white doves? Do not toy with your beloved! I carry your son!"

Such lies she told and others: that he wandered at night upon the cliffs howling like a wild dog, that he ate raw venison upon the heath, that he took her again and again on nights when the moon rose full as he called out profanely to the shaking trees.

Lies! The Devil's lies! He was now so weakened he could barely walk from the door of the church to the altar.

One night, not long after the boy was born, Blackwell awoke to find Rosemary gone. In each of his hands there lay curled a green snake! The terrible creatures danced and hissed within his grasp. The Devil mocking him!

Under the bright moon he felt suddenly strong and filled with a righteous rage. He threw the snakes to the floor and crushed them beneath his boot then ran to gather water at the stream. He had not felt such strength in years! Several more serpents trailed him down the path, but he crushed all he could beneath his boot and cursed even the moonlight (for its silver rays were like snakes writhing in the sky!).

He did as the one-eyed hag had told him. He set the water boiling and took up a silver dagger. Two snakes appeared again upon the threshold and he cut them asunder. He cut a great lock of hair from his beard and threw the coil to the steam. He stared down at his reflection in the steaming pot and cried, "Reveal witch! Reveal thy face!"

Lo! Who came rushing through the door, dragged by the force of her own evil, dragged by great winds from some infernal black mass under the trees?

There Rosemary stood with green snakes wrapped about her naked thighs and grass stains upon her bare buttocks. She laughed like a lunatic and claimed she had only returned from chasing a fox out of the hen house!

Yes, how merrily she laughed, not knowing she was revealed by the one-eyed hag's spell to be the tormenter of his soul.

***

That terrible May evening...

They sat on the shores of Lake Twilight and Blackwell sang love songs to her accompanied by a spruce-wood lute.

"Rosemary," he whispered when he set down his instrument at last. "Rosemary, my heart aches as if it is broken already. 'Tis madness, I know, for here you are right beside me."

"Please," she answered, smoothing down the skirt of her velvet dress. "Let us be happy and not worry of what is to be."

"I cannot." Blackwell answered. "I cannot! Nothing in this world may be held for more than an instant before time rips it from our grasp! Can you feel the seconds fall away? It is unbearable to know that this night must end so that others may unfold even if the days to come prove better. 'Tis agony, this great pleasure I take in your company! It would have been kinder if the Lord had struck me down the very moment I first spied you in the thicket!"

A single tear fell down Blackwell's cheek as he spoke and Rosemary took the silver drop upon her finger and brought it to her lips.

His tear was sweet! Like dew gathered on an apple blossom. Her whole body quivered with the pleasure of it. She turned away to hide the shameful hunger that rose in her as his sadness slid down her parched throat and her trembling tongue licked its memory from her lips.

Oh! What barely caged sin lurked within her! She lusted, yes, lusted, even for the tears falling from her lover's eye!

She ran from Blackwell. She ran and ran, trampling over the fields of blooming night lilies and up into the oak forest. She feared greatly what would happened if she remained. She did not want to kiss Blackwell. She did not want to lay with him gently in the shaded groves of purple heather. No! She wanted to ravage him, like a starving hawk tearing apart a mouse with beak and claw, leaving nothing save a twist of hair and a pile of gnawed bones!

She ran and ran and, though she heard Blackwell follow for a time, eventually he lost her trail. He circled the green valley while she climbed higher into the forest. Deep into the shadowed trees she ran where she had never dared to venture before (for there were witches living in hollowed logs here that made soup from the bones of lost children and wandering huntsmen).

In her madness Rosemary ran through the endless bramble and briar, screaming up at the twisted, leafless branches and feeling herself utterly overtaken by lust. A roe fawn leapt across her path and she remembered nothing more...

In the rosy dawn, she came back to herself and found she was lying in a grove of newly toppled birch trees. Her beautiful velvet dress was stained with splatters of dark mud and torn beyond repair. Her hands were scratched and blood-stained and, oh, oh... In her arms there lay the roe fawn with its neck twisted.

* * *

There he stood by the dark hearth with the water rolling and spitting so that his reflection looked that of a monster as the moonlight fell upon the boiling pot. Snakes writhed up from the steam and Rosemary laughed merrily.

"Husband!" She cried. "Do not look so angrily upon your loving wife!"

He took up the iron poker and raised it above his head. A great hailstorm came tumbling upon the roof. Her little dog rose and danced upon its two back legs and terrible clots of blood pooled upon the floor.

Such agonies went through him as he came toward her. Hail-stones pounded like war drums upon the roof and blood spread across the floor as the little dancing dog howled (and Rosemary cried, "Husband! Lover! Stay thy hand!"). The sky flashed white as he dealt her a grievous blow upon the head.

She fell and remained senseless as he dragged her up the mountain. The dog followed, whimpering in the darkness as Blackwell prayed to the Lord, "Stay my hand! Stay my hand!"

Yet even as Rosemary awoke upon the last bend in the path and struggled like a wild thing to be free of him, Blackwell felt strong and filled with the light of God, but there was no sound save Rosemary's scream as she beheld his dagger.

The Lord remained silent.

Thus Blackwell slew his wife (and the dog, and several tawny rabbits, and two gray squirrels he spied upon his way down the hill). If God did not listen then the Devil surely did, yet neither deigned to speak.

Now Blackwell slid from the sky, still lost in his sea fever. He slid down to the water, down to the ship, down to his body where it lay upon the cabin floor. He tried to reach out to take his son's hand, to grab a hammer, to kill them both, but he could not stop his sliding down. He slid right through himself and down, down farther. He sunk through the ship, through the nests of rats in the dark joists between the decks (licking furiously at each other's fur and whispering, "We shall live! We shall live!").

Down he fell through the groaning hull of the ship, down into the silent depths of the sea. He heard the cold laugh of the ocean and the empty, loveless chorus of the fish who swam its darkest depths where no light had ever shone.

Blackwell shivered, feeling the utter coldness of this place. He watched as each black fish gaped its slimy jaw to devour another, one after the next. What a great chain of death he saw stretching backward to the beginning of time and forward to its end! He followed it, not knowing if he went backward or forward, not knowing how long he traveled (though it seemed so long a time that there were no words for it and, indeed, he forgot many of the words he had learned and even the word that was his own name) until, at long last, he found himself again returned to his body...

The Governor's men could find no proof of his wife's murder. Still, they put him in leg screws and thumb screws and flogged him time and again. He confessed nothing (though he was terribly burned with heated shovels and pricked all over with pins as the Governor's men searched for a sign of his pact with the Devil).

Finally it was said that Rosemary ran away with a tinker from the lowlands. But, lo! Now the Governor was visited by great swellings upon his legs and the man's ankles grew so large he could not walk. Black flies swarmed about his bilious limbs and he could not leave his manor without a retinue of servants to fan the air about him.

From his silk-sheeted bed the Governor called for the killing of all black sheep and spotted calves. Yet the man's pain only increased and his swollen legs grew so large and tender he could do naught but lay in his vast four-posted bed and scream up at the frescoed ceiling.

Now the Governor called for the cutting down of all rowan trees and for all gypsies and Jews to be thrown to the river. Still his pain worsened. He called for all blind people and for those with crooked limbs to be thrown to the fires. The pain grew unbearable and it seemed he could do naught save whimper from dawn to dusk. Finally he called for the dunking of witches.

Now neighbor turned upon neighbor and many were accused. Countless screaming innocents were dragged to the courthouse. Seldom did any return. At last, the guards came for Blackwell. Lo! When he was carried before the Governor, the great man's ankles burst. Blood poured forth in such a stream of agonies that the ailing man saw yellow birds flying circles about his head and he heard the very Devil laughing in his ear! In the midst of such anguish the Governor pointed his finger at Blackwell and cried out, "'Tis thee, sir! Thee!"

And Blackwell, seeing the foolish man shuddering in fear and pain, made no denial. He demanded lands and freedom.

"Else," Blackwell cried, "I shall bring such pestilence upon this town that ye shall all beg for death. Give me what I ask for or you shall drown in blood running like a river from your mouth!"

He was given passage to the new world and he rejoiced (for he was sure he would be rid of her if only he journeyed far enough away).

✝ ✝ ✝

Such a storm of bitterness poured out from Rosemary as she lay dying upon the rocks that she heard it screaming and echoing far out across the mountains (and even down, down, miles down, into the darkness under the sea where silver fish fled in terrified clouds of glitter).

Such a howl came forth from her that there was left behind a great empty place inside her heart. A cavern opened within her very soul and it was shaped like the word "No!"

From this lightless, frozen maw a terrible creature wriggled free. The creature was ancient and foul. Its icy claws were like a fire upon her skin. Slowly it crept down her shivering breast. She felt utterly helpless. She howled a wordless shriek as the creature nuzzled against her, cold as death, blindly searching with its hideous mouth. Its frozen teeth bit fiercely upon her teat and it began to suckle.

Now a great clattering began. A toad fell from the sky then another and another. A rain of toads fell about her. Huge black toads, small white ones, glistening brown ones coated with slime, golden toads with black eyes, green toads with long delicate fingers tipped in red...The toads fell faster and faster, chirping in panic as they fell and hopping madly in all directions, trying to free themselves from the mounting pile.

Rosemary screamed and screamed. Still the toads thundered down and many a toad was crushed by the ones that followed. There was a great writhing mass of toads pushing and pulling with all their strength to climb free of each other. The living toads crawled upon the mountains of the dead, so that they were all splattered and smeared with blood.

These filthy toads spread out across her body and suckled upon every exposed inch of her skin. Their tiny mouths, cold and hungry, pulled at her from every direction and she was sure they would tear her apart. Worst of all was the little demon at her breast that sucked so fiercely upon her it seemed to suck away everything she had ever possessed.

Still, the grievous wound at her neck had closed and she felt strong enough to smash a ship with her fist.

In the darkness she heard Blackwell return. He knelt at her side and his smile revealed sharp white teeth. He kissed her with such abandon she felt utterly blinded by it. They rolled upon the bodies of the dead and dying toads and she did not care that the blood of fallen toads splattered upon her flesh or that she was covered in small, bleeding cuts or that her lover tore away her clothing and kissed her naked breast with a mouth full of sharp teeth, cold as the snow.

She dug her nails into the fur of his back and wound her bare feet tightly about his long and powerful limbs. She pressed her tongue and the edges of her teeth to the black fur of his neck and she tasted his blood in her mouth. He was howling and panting in her ear and his barbed tail beat against her thigh.

Far below her, in a tiny sea, she saw a ship turned over in the water and people, small as ants, floundering in the waves. She laughed and clung tighter to the beast.

***

Now, in the great dark depths of night, Blackwell began to hear voices echoing across the ocean waves: crying children, screaming women, the wild whoop of savages. He lay with his heart pounding and tears glistening in his eyes as the senseless din roared about him. In the midst of this wondrous cacophony, the cabin door swung open.

Rosemary returned. She flew into the room in a rush of sea wind. She wore nothing save a long winding sheet that trailed out the door into the breeze. Under the moon's light Blackwell saw the outline of her naked form beneath the gauzy sheet as she glided into the cabin and lay herself upon him.

He found he could not move or cry out. Rosemary lay upon him with such a force he could not even breathe. He was desperate for air, but he could no longer move or see. He felt her warm body (her round hips and full breasts) pressing and rubbing against him so that even as he felt himself suffocating he could not help but feel a surge of shameful lust.

Rosemary's red lips pressed hot and wet against his own. Her tongue pushed into his mouth so deeply it seemed to suck the very life from him. A great flash of light revealed her face before him and she was ancient: a wizened creature, toothless and wrinkled with only darkness where one of her eyes should have been. With a deafening cackle, the one-eyed hag drank the last gasp of air from his lungs and he knew nothing more.

When he opened his eyes again he found that he was in the water. The ship was on its side and all around him the passengers screamed and struggled and drowned. A great hand pulled against him as the ship sunk beneath the waves so that he could do naught but follow it to the depths.

A vision unfolded as he drowned. He saw the far shore. He saw air ships gliding from the clouds in trails of smoke. He saw steaming horseless carriages winding over mountaintops and rivers spanned by enormous silver bridges.

He watched as the verdant forests and golden beaches, the herds of buffalo, and the flocks of birds were all taken up in smoke. He saw the land wiped clean and death, beautiful death, taking into its mouth everything green and blooming, panting and leaping, until nothing remained but silence.

He saw a great city, cold and pale, where trees were planted in rows. Fences circled hills. Rivers were dammed and still. He saw a world tamed and tethered. He saw a room, clean and white, utterly bare and silent. He entered it and fell to his knees, weeping with joy. At last he was in Heaven.

It was this clean white room that he had lusted for all his life and he understood that, in her own way, Rosemary had also longed for this cold, silent place (for there she was in the corner, standing perfectly still on a square of white silk). This room was called Death and it was holy.

He saw all this as he sank beneath the sea and he cried, "Hallelujah!" as the ocean rushed into his mouth.

None heard his cry (save the little fish nibbling his dead fingers and the brown mud below, waiting to take his body into her arms).

Pecan Trees Are Self Pruning
★
BY JIM WHITE

Trouble today. The old car I was driving broke down. Again. It's
sitting across the way, there on the far side of the road. Steaming.
Hissing. Offering up the occasional metallic moan. I'm in the
middle of nowhere. I walk the shoulder for a while then meander
over to a long forgotten pecan grove down the way. Weeds and
scrub oak have overtaken the tumbledown fence. Tacked to the
nearest pecan tree is a crude, hand painted sign that reads:

Danger??? Falling limbs??

It's a gray, wintry day, but a brief burst of sunlight strafes
the sign just so, imbuing it with a worrisome valence. It momentarily glows. As I stand there some fifty feet off I'm hit with a
sudden, intense urge to steal this sign, to go fetch my lug wrench
from the car, pry it off that tree, and take it with me. I shake my
head in wonder at my own stupidity. Why even consider such
senseless petty theft? What use would I have for that sign? Back
when I was a kid I'd indulge myself in the occasional incidental
crime of opportunity, but I'm a grown man now and when you're
grown you have to act more reasonable. You can't just go around
stealing everything that strikes your fancy.

I chide myself some more like this but when I run out of chides I still want to steal the damn sign. It's the middle of nowhere, no town in sight, not a soul around. So what if I was to remove this one forgotten sign? Who would miss it? What's the worst that could happen? If I was caught would I even get jail time? Likely not. And what are the odds of some vigilante pecan farmer with a squirrel rifle hiding in the tall grass, just waiting for my long fettered criminal impulses to suddenly break through?

None.

I survey the area for onlookers or possible traps, then take a step closer.

Now I realize why I want to steal the sign—so I can give it to that waitress back home. She's a freewheeling type and easy on the eyes and haven't I been looking for a good "in" with her? What would she do if I was to come knocking on her door late some night? Tell her to hold out her hands and close her eyes, then present her with this weird sign? Would she give me a giddy, sparkly eyed look and come tumbling into my arms, or gawk at me like I've got three heads?

The old car sighs, then grows silent; sleeping, perhaps dead. That's it. It's the waitress I want the sign for. It's not for myself. It's for her that I step closer to study the sign further. There's something about that crooked arrow that I like—how it first underscores the three words, then aims upward, toward the heavens, helpfully describing the exact direction from whence said deadly limbs might fall. It feels like the exclamation point to some exotic joke I don't get but wish I did. The sign's about ten feet off now and everything about it is just so appealing. The more I see it, the more I want to steal it. But I know it's wrong to steal so I walk off, farther into the tangle of trees.

The false silence of the pecan grove becomes disquieting. It's a cold, windy day and the swaying trees are all stripped bare. There's an ebb and flow of gentle whooshing as the gusts buffet the higher limbs. It sounds sort of like waves on the shoreline, which should be calming but isn't. I guess it's the peril of those falling limbs...

Danger??? Falling limbs??

Though I've seen pecan trees all my life it suddenly occurs to me that they're strangely configured. I stare up at the network of lopsided branches crisscrossing the sky nonsensically, twisting to and fro in a manner that seems to contradict various fundamental laws of physics. No wonder the damn limbs fall. Helter-skelter engineering like this can't much agree with the larger ordinances of that eternal menace, gravity.

I feel a chill coming on. I should get. Leave the sign where it is and just go. Buy the waitress a funny T-shirt or something. But where the hell am I? What's the closest town? Is it thirty miles to Calhoun? To Mount Olive? To Seminary? It doesn't much matter. In the coming hours I'll walk some distance, to some town or other. I'll find some mechanic with some old tow truck. On the way to fetch the car he'll offer me pearls of wisdom or tales of woe or one of fifty variations of the old small-town auto repair hustle. These certainties I can rest my head upon, like a pillowcase stuffed full of old shoes and silverware.

I turn to leave, then look back at the sign. There it is again—the urge to steal. It's not just the waitress, is it? I want this sign for me. But why? It's something about the lettering—I mean, what disposition of hand would paint letters that way? A sane, sensible hand? No. More than likely it's the trembling hand of some lunatic, some redneck Chicken Little fighting a losing battle with dementia. That's the most likely possibility. But impending madness isn't necessarily a liability, now is it? What if, in his skirmish with mental instability, the sign painter stumbled upon something essential—some secret that escapes casual inspection, that reveals tantalizing mysteries about the world behind the world?

Danger??? Falling Limbs??

It's not just the lettering, or even the caddywhompass shape of the board; there's also something odd about the wording. I mean, why pose a certainty as a question? This grove is scattered with fallen limbs, so limbs will fall, have fallen since the dawn of time by the evidence all around, and falling things of that size will certainly pose magnitudes of danger to anyone or thing beneath them as they come down. So why the question marks? (???) It makes me wonder again; am I really seeing what the sign painter intended me to see, or am I missing some crucial point—some hidden joke? But if there's a hidden joke, then who's the joker? The sign painter? God? The waitress? Those little pumps that control chemical balances in my brain? Damn this sign. I step closer to examine it more closely. Scrape-scrape-scrape. Tap-tap-tap. Just wood and paint with one rusty nail holding it in place. Hell, with a good swift yank it'd come down. I wouldn't even need the lug wrench.I give it a brief exploratory tug and down it comes. So there it is. I'm holding the sign now, studying the feel of it. Suddenly the phrase "aesthetic outburst" appears in the midnight sky of my mind, like a pretty fireworks explosion. I've not heard or used that phrase before, yet it makes sense when applied to the puzzle of the sign.

Aesthetic outburst. Does that mean that when the sign was being painted, unbeknownst to the sign painter, a mysterious charge attached itself to the final product, like some mischievous chimera? Probably.

There's the sound of a truck coming, then slowing. I drop the sign and quickly shuffle away, distancing myself from it like some dumb kid caught with his hand in the cookie jar. A shiny Step Van emblazoned with the Snap-On Tools logo pulls up alongside the old car. The driver gets out and hollers, looking around for me I guess, then he ducks his head under the opened hood. He hasn't seen me yet, so I kick some leaves over the sign, then step out from behind the tree and call out, "Hey!" The Snap-On man peeks around the hood and tips his ball cap at me. He's poking around in the engine when I get up there.

"Broke down?" he asks.

I yep him. We swap names. He's Ronnie Skipper.

"What's she doing?" Ronnie asks, using that interested tone that men who know cars and love working on them use.

"It's been running rough for a while now. It started sputtering and missing real bad this morning. About a mile back it overheated. I was trying to make it to the next town. See if there was a mechanic."

"Oh, you don't want him," he says matter-of-factly, still studying the engine. "Mind if I take a look?"

"Help yourself." I say.

He fishes a Leatherman out of his back pocket, pops the top of the distributor off, pokes around for a second, then starts laughing. He points out a device about the size of a half-dollar sitting to one side of the interior of the distributor. "It's your points..." he tells me, working free the center screw and lifting the small device out. "See that little hammer? When it hits, a spark is supposed to jump across the gap. But look..." There is no gap. The tip of the hammer and the platform it's supposed to strike are both covered with small calcified carbon lumps.

"Look at that. It's a miracle she ran at all." He scratches at the lump with his fingernail then wipes his hands on a rag he's got dangling from his back pocket. "I got business up in Castleberry. You can ride with me if you want. We can pick you up some points at Enfingers." He reaches to pull the hood down but stops midway. "Might as well check the plugs, too," he says. He fetches an extension socket wrench from his truck and eases out the plugs, revealing one by one tips that should have a fine machined look to them, but instead are covered in black gunk. He just shakes his head.

"I bet them Arabs like you," he says, patting the car. "All the go-juice you been sucking down." I smile sheepishly, thinking about the small fortune I've spent recently on gas.

As we're riding to town I ask him about the pecan grove.

"Back there? I picked pecans in that field a few times. Good-sized Stuarts. But it's all run down now."

"What happened? Did the farmer die or something?"

"I don't know. When I was a kid it was well tended, but nobody looks after it any more. It's shame, all them good pecans going to waste in the long grass. Was that what you were doing?" he asks. "Hunting pecans?"

"Naw. I was just killing time until the radiator cooled down. I was over there looking at that sign."

"What sign?"

"It was tacked to one of the trees. It said, 'Danger, falling limbs.'" I don't bother to enumerate the eccentricities of the sign, as I figure it's unlikely they'd make much sense to Ronnie.

"Yeah, pecan trees, they're self pruning," he says. "Limbs get too heavy, they just break off and fall. Day like today, with that wind, you got to be mindful of what's above you. There's folks that have been killed by branches falling."

"Is that a fact?"

"Yes it is," Ronnie says. "One minute they're standing there picking pecans, the next minute they're stone cold dead." Ronnie pauses, letting that image sink in, then says, "Of course, you never know when your time is up, do you?"

"Nope." I say.

Now, his friendly mechanic delivery modulates slightly to a more clumsy, paternal tone. "Death comes like a thief in the night. It does. It makes you think about where you might spend eternity…" There's a long, awkward pause, then finally Ronnie looks over at me and earnestly inquires, "How about you? Do you know where you'll spend eternity?"

I guess I should have seen this coming. Ronnie's so cleancut. He works on cars but hasn't asked for money or said the word bitch or made any off-color jokes in our conversation thus far. He's probably imagining himself as that Samaritan who helped Jesus in the Bible, and he's not far off. He's come to my aid and I'm truly grateful for that. But after all these years of getting jumped by Christian muggers every time I so much as try to buy a stick of gum, I tend to get touchy about good will that turns out to be foreplay for proselytizing. Like a friend of mine once said, "Nothing is purer than the kindness of an atheist."

"I'm already spending eternity," I say. "I died years ago and this place is where they sent me." I smile contentedly at Ronnie, who looks confused.

"So, this place you been sent..." he says. "Is it heaven or is it hell?"

"That's the part I haven't figured out yet."

Ronnie nods, "Well, if you're searching for answers, I know of someone who can help." he says. I ignore the bait, but he continues. "His name is Jesus."

I figure it's time to nip this in the bud.

"I'm not really in the market for answers, Ronnie," I say. "See, me and answers we had a big fight a while back. We don't talk much anymore. These days I mostly keep company with questions."

Ronnie frowns slightly, confused again by my evasive, flowery talk, which is understandably an unpleasant foreign language to him. As he mulls over my response, the image of all those question marks on the pecan sign suddenly flashes in my mind and I smile. A certainty posed as a question...maybe that's why I wanted that damn sign so much.

Danger??? Falling limbs??

Ronnie falls silent, as do I. A mile passes without much more being said. Then another, then another. As the rows of planted pine trees go whizzing by I imagine myself happily lost in a vast expanse of them, each and every one looming over me like a huge, rough-hewn question mark.

We come to the town of Castleberry. I figure I'm gonna get dumped at some garage but Ronnie sticks by my side. We hit Enfingers Auto Supply and pick up some plugs and a distributor kit. It sets me back a mere twenty-five bucks, thanks to Ronnie's professional discount. Ronnie drops off a floor jack and set of torque wrenches a few blocks away at Larcomb Motors, a used-car place that doubles as a repair shop, then insists on driving me back out to my car.

He doesn't mention Jesus again. We make small talk along the way as he shows me how to gap the plugs and set up the distributor. He's married, has three young sons, and grew up in Castleberry but now lives twenty miles to the north in the town where his wife is from. His territory is a hundred and seventy-five miles square and he drives an average of two hundred miles a day. His daddy taught him how to work on cars and when time permits he stops to help out stranded motorists like me.

I tell him a little about my life; how I'm a musician and where I'm from. When I mention I got no wife or kids this seems to cause him no end of puzzlement.

"So it's just you alone in the world?" he asks.

"Pretty much," I say.

He shakes his head in bewilderment.

The plugs and points are set and Ronnie locks the distributor cap back in place. I give the ignition key a twist and that old car cranks right up, running smooth for the first time since I got it two years prior. It's a good sound. A billowing gray cloud of smoke fills the air momentarily—all that excess gas and crud being burned off. I offer to pay him for his time but Ronnie the good Christian refuses. We shake hands and he heads off to his truck.

A second later he comes trotting back and offers me a Chicklet, one of those bizarre little Christian comic books. This one is called That Was Your Life! It's about a godless man who dies and is taken to heaven. There, to his horror and shame, before God and the host of angels, his miserable sin-filled life is replayed. Then he's cast out of heaven into the fires of hell, where he's greeted by a sneering devil with horns, a long barbed tail, and a trident.

As I'm flipping through the book Ronnie lays his hand on my shoulder. "What about now?" he says. "Does that make you think about where you'll spend eternity?" Despite his ham-fisted evangelizing, I like Ronnie. He's a simple, kind person who believes in a literal heaven and hell and sincerely worries for my eternal soul, and while normally this kind of witnessing gets me so fired up I get to shouting and gesticulating wildly, with Ronnie I don't mind. I just smile and study his peaceful countenance. I don't have the heart to try to debate with him or contaminate his simple faith with my convoluted notions of metaphysics. I can't get any madder at him than I could some lovely, well-meaning child who's gravely warning me about the imaginary monster hiding under his bed.

"Thanks again for the help," I say, trying to evade further awkwardness. But Ronnie's a dog with a bone.

"Will you do me a favor?" he says.

"I will if I can," I say.

"I've got a Bible up in the truck. There's a passage I want you to read. It's in John—verse 3:16. Will you read that with me?"

I smile at Ronnie, close my eyes, and say, "Better yet: For God so loved the world that he gave his only begotten son that whosoever should believe in him would not perish but have everlasting life. John 3:16." I open my eyes and smile at Ronnie, who looks slightly startled. I guess he took me for a heathen.

"Hell, everyone knows that one Ronnie," I say.

He studies me for a moment then gives me a pained, tender smile. "You've been close to the Lord before, haven't you?' he says softly. "What happened? How did you drift so far away?"

"I don't know, Ronnie. I guess I'm like a pecan tree. One day that limb just couldn't bear the weight any more and it fell off."

Ronnie thinks this over and says, "It's not like that. Jesus is the tree. It was you that fell away. And you can run all you want, but no matter how far you go, Jesus is always right there beside you. Every mile of the way. Open your heart and listen. You'll hear it; that still small voice calling out your name. That's the Lord, looking for one of his lost sheep. That's Jesus... looking for you. When you're driving, will you promise me you'll open your heart... and listen for his voice?"

"Okay, Ronnie. I'll give it a try," I say.

"I'll be praying for you."

"Okay. Suit yourself," I say.

After Ronnie pulls away I grab my lug wrench from the trunk and walk over to the pecan grove. The sign's still there. It looks so sad and purposeless lying in the weeds where I left it. I do my best to tack it back up to the tree, but a lug wrench isn't a hammer, now is it? Between the yank I gave it and the agents of time and gravity, the nail is too far gone. What to do? Regardless of ownership, it just doesn't seem right to just abandon it here in the tall grass to rot among myriad forgotten pecans limbs.So I'm back to square one. There's not a soul around. Not a car in sight. In the end I slip it under my coat, head back up to the car, and stash it in the trunk. I feel like I just robbed Fort Knox. I hit the highway, heading north for Nashville. Thirty miles along I intersect I-55 and though I prefer riding the back roads, to make up for lost time I jump into the stream of speeding semis and SUVs. A few hours later I take a break, filling the tank at truck stop near a town called Senatobia. Ronnie was right, those bad points and plugs were killing my gas mileage. In just a few short hours I've already made up the money I spent fixing the car.

As I'm hopping back on I-55, right there at the off-ramp there's a hitchhiker. He's not some scruffy hippie with a sympathy dog or a wino or a serial killer type. He's a young guy with a bedroll atop a well-tended hiker's backpack. He looks like he ought to be in college. It's gone cold as hell outside and though these days I tend to not pick up strangers, I size this one up and decide to give him the benefit of the doubt. Likely it's some legacy of Ronnie's kindness. The kid looks relieved when I pull over. He tells me he's headed out west, to Colorado.

"You picked a hell of a time of year to be hitch-hiking across the Midwest," I say, "You must want to get somewhere pretty bad."

"I do," he says softly, "I'm looking for my wife and little girl. " He gazes out the window, a portrait of regret. "They took off last summer. She's got a sister in Boulder, so I figured I'd go there first."

"Why'd they run off?"

He sighs. "It's my own damn fault. I started smoking that rock cocaine and couldn't stop. I got crazy and popped her a few times. The next day she was gone. Took the kids and the car. Two weeks later I got busted for possession and did six months. I don't ever want to go back to prison."

He talks briefly about his stay in jail, then falls into a deep sleep. It's nearing midnight and a gentle snow is falling when I let him out at that off-ramp on the outskirts of Memphis where I-40 and I-55 meet up. He'll go west and I'll go east. I shake his hand and wish him good luck. As he steps out into the night and I ease away, I can't help but notice the palpable sense of terror in his eyes as he forlornly waves goodbye.

With nothing but open highway before me, I hit the gas and am surprised how the engine purrs, then lifts in response. I can't help but think about Ronnie and his kindness to me and that promise I made to him. I try to keep my promises, no matter how absurd they might be, so as the old car plunges forward into the empty darkness, though I know it's a fool's errand, I decide to open my heart and listen for that still small voice he spoke of.

For a while there's nothing but the hush within and the dark roaring highway hurtling by outside, but slowly a sense of weightlessness begins to overtake me and I feel as though I am rising into the thin air. I see the old car from above, as if I'm flying over it, then rise farther, into the clouds, then above the whole of the earth. I see fallow fields and signs with unknown meanings. I see goodness and mercy and pride and sin all hopelessly entangled with the will to power. I see sparks jumping ragged gaps, and deadly limbs forever poised to fall from on high. I see every foolish place I've been, and every harebrained scheme I've thought up and marvel at the fantastic shapes that time and circumstance can twist a person into and suddenly realize that every one of us is born to grow so full of proud improbabilities that under the simple weight of living, pieces of our being must from time to time collapse and fall into the loving arms of gravity. For if God is nothing else, it is gravity... and what falls upon us depends so much upon how low we've sunk when that which is above us gives way.

I'm awakened from my reverie when, from out of the dark highway behind me, I see a pair of headlights closing fast in the rear view mirror. I look down—my speedometer's pegged at a hundred and twenty miles per hour. Who could it be chasing me at such speeds? Is it God? The sign painter? The waitress? Ronnie? Who could it be?

Then the blue lights flash and the siren wails. I think of the stolen sign in the trunk and I start laughing. If this is the voice of God, that's just fine by me.

The Bird Feeder

★

BY LAURA VEIRS

Mr. Jackson rapped his cane on the living room window. The squirrels were stealing the birdseed again. They used to scatter when he rapped at them but now they just packed their cheeks and stared. His neck flushed and he unbuttoned the top button of his shirt. He settled himself in his chair and looked over at the TV.

He never imagined he'd end up like this. A sad old man living alone in a crumbling house, walking around with a cane, his social life consisting of playing gin-rummy with Jim and Robert every Wednesday night, and his wife dead. Dear Leena. For forty-six years they'd lived together, traveled the world, raised two kids, and retired to the Ohio countryside. Then her body sucked into itself and her lungs filled with fluid and she left him lying cold and lonely in an empty bed. The day she died he cried a flash flood and watched his heart fly up to the heavens to try and find her.

Since her death his mouth had turned in on itself like a prune and his eyes, watery and topaz-colored, were strangely blank. Wild white hairs grew from his brows, his skin peppered with dark brown spots. He'd always tapped his fingers as a nervous habit, but now he wrung his hands to hide their involuntary trembling.

The house was falling down around him. The roof leaked, the kitchen sink dripped, the porch stairs were rotting, and the yard was a mess. Thick ropes of morning glory twisted through the vegetable patch. His children came to help now and then but they lived on the West Coast and led busy lives. They tried to arrange for outside help but he wouldn't have it. He kept up with the minimum of tasks, ate simple meals, and spent his days watching TV infomercials.

After two years he still hadn't dealt with Leena's things. Her closet full of clothes. Her half-done canvases standing in the family room. Her mother-of-pearl comb, still resting on her bedside table, woven with long white strands. Her pack of Winstons collecting dust on the piano bench.

One afternoon a particular infomercial had caught his attention. It showed beautiful children delighting in a variety of birds that pecked playfully at a feeder outside. Their cute blonde mother turned to the camera and smiled.

—For only $39.99, this feeder and a two-month supply of birdseed could be yours. You, too, can experience the entertainment of the natural world in the comfort of your own home!

He remembered the birds and the feeder outside Leena's window at the hospital. She loved watching them but could only identify the cardinals, sparrows, and blue jays. He'd bought her a hardback color version of *American Songbirds*. When she wasn't sleeping, which was most of the time, she was telling him about their songs, their migration patterns, their mating habits.

He considered the woman on the TV. The last thing he'd ordered was a collection of old country hits which were disappointingly sappy. Leena would have liked them, though. Before that he'd ordered an air freshener set with different scents: mint, lime, lavender, and rosemary. She was always spraying those around to mask the smell of her cigarettes. The house still smelled but he never used the air fresheners; he preferred to leave the windows open if it wasn't too cold.

He wondered if he should give up on the infomercials. Still, he wrote down the number and ordered the feeder. It arrived the next week. He set it up, sat down heavily in his easy chair, and waited.

Within a day the word was out. Baltimore orioles, blue jays, cedar waxwings, and yellow-throated flycatchers streaked across the sky, back and forth to the fire-colored maple trees. The cardinals were his favorite. Sometimes he tried to whistle their complicated songs.

It didn't take long before the squirrels swarmed the feeder. Refilling it became more and more difficult as the cold weather moved in. He had to bundle up and take extra care on the back porch stairs where ice formed. Sometimes he missed a day. The birds went elsewhere.

He went to the hardware store and brought home five rat-traps. He set them on the kitchen table. Wisps of his hair fell across his forehead as he studied their powerful steel parts and heavy-duty springs. He imagined pulling a squirrel out of the trap. It'd be better to throw the whole thing away, trap and squirrel and all. He remembered the time when he was a boy and his father set a mousetrap in the living room before bed.

— We've got a serious problem with all these mice in the house. Don't worry if you hear this thing go off in the night. I'll take care of it in the morning.

That night he lay drifting off to sleep when the trap snapped. He sat up in bed and listened. Outside, the sky was a field of black. He got up, turned on the living room light, and walked over to the trap. He crouched down and looked at it. A muted brown mouse with its neck snapped. Its tongue out, its long front teeth bared, its eyes black and surprised. There was a spray of blood on the floor. He shuddered and went back to his room. It took forever to fall asleep. When he got up in the morning the trap was gone and his father didn't mention it.

The next night his father set it again, and again a snap from the living room. He hesitated but he got up. The expression on this mouse's face was oddly serene. Its blood pooled on the wood of the trap. He gulped and went to bed and slept fitfully.

It happened again the next night. But this time the mouse was alive and squeaking. Its front shoulder was caught and its head was partially crushed. It was flinging its tail and haunches from side to side. Its one eye was bulging, brown and bright and horrible. He thought there were some brains on the wood but he didn't really want to look. He stood back and watched as the thrashing weakened. One final swish of the tail and it was dead.

He raised a shaky hand to his temple. Black dots appeared and disappeared at the edges of his vision. He turned off the living room light. A nightlight cast a sick yellow glow across the floor. He stopped and steadied himself. Took a deep breath. The refrigerator made a clunky sound and then stopped. Dad will take care of this. Dad knows best. *There's always an efficient solution, son.* He wiped his hands on his pajama bottoms and went back to his room.

The next morning he said nothing to his father. That night he lay awake for hours, waiting for the dreaded snap. It never came. In the dim pink light of morning he finally slept. After breakfast his father put the stained trap—spattered and black with blood—back in its box.

— Guess we got 'em all for now.

— Guess so.

That night he went out to set the traps. A cold breeze rattled leaves around on the grass. A carnival of stars lit up the sky. He strained and pulled the metal hinges apart. He baited them with cheese, went inside, and slept.

In the morning he woke up sweating. Someone was knocking on the back door. He struggled into his clothes, grabbed his cane, smoothed the hair over his bald spot, and opened the door. One of the neighbor girls was standing on the porch. She was about fifteen years old; he didn't remember her name. Her skin was pimply and inflamed. Her thin black shirt said REM on it. She squinted up at him.

— Mr. Jackson, have you seen any kittens in your backyard? I was playing with the whole litter this morning but one's gone missing.

A jolt in his chest. He licked his lips and took a deep breath.

— No, I haven't. What's your name again?

— Clara.

She had dyed black hair, knotty and disheveled.

— I'll keep an eye out for him. What does he look like?

— She. She's gray with green eyes.

She blew a huge purple bubble. It popped on her face and she pulled it off and put it back in her mouth.

— Her name's Sylvia. Short for Sylvia Plath? Definitely my favorite poet. But I have to give up all but one for adoption next week and I think I'm going to keep the black one who is called Nina. After Nina Simone? Definitely my favorite singer.

She chewed her gum hard and twisted her finger in her hair.

He started to close the door.

— I'll be sure to look out for her.

She stopped him.

— Can I look in your backyard?

He paused, considering. The blue of her eyes. He couldn't just tell her to go home. She picked at a scab on her arm. He hoped the kitten was playing happily somewhere.

— Hang on. I'll get my coat.

Outside, he watched as a maple leaf landed on the yellowing grass. The air smelled of rotting apples. The pond was full of scum and the flowers were dead and the hedges were overgrown. Clara stooped and pulled twigs out of her woolly red leg warmers.

— Clara, look under the steps here.

His eyes flitted about the yard while she crawled under the back porch. She came out and dusted off her knees. He sent her in the opposite direction.

— You look that way, behind the garage and inside it. If you don't find her, look around the rocks by the pond. I'll check the trees. OK?

— K.

It didn't take him long to find the kitten crying in one of the traps. Her front right leg had snapped, the bone poking through like a cracked pink toothpick, her gray fur a mangled mess of blood and bone. Burrs lodged in the fur between the pads of the toes. Her eyes were green and fierce, her pupils black slits. She struggled to free herself, growling low and guttural.

Electricity bolted through him as he knelt down and tried not to look. He squinted his eyes. His hands shook wildly as he pulled open the trap. Blood on his hands, on her fur, on the trap. Her bad paw dangling on a thin red string. He tried to hold her but she twisted and bit his hands. She growled and her claws dug into him. He pushed her down between two old roots and stood up.

He put a trembling, bloody hand to his shirt. His lungs were tight, like he was breathing underwater. He couldn't make his arms pick her up again. Inky spots pooled at the sides of his eyes. The bark on the tree moved leopard-like. He didn't know how to help.

As if watching from the top of the canopy, he saw himself walk to the opposite side of the tree. He thought about Leena in her wool cardigan with her cigarette and bourbon and her beautiful white hair. Her final paintings all different kinds of blue. Blue bottles, blue pears, blue beach scenes, blue hyacinths. Leena in the garden, Leena canning berries, Leena mending clothes, Leena cutting his hair.

He looked up and saw her standing in the yard. She was wearing her gardening clothes. Her face was smudged with dirt. Smoke rose from her cigarette in a thin purple plume.

— My heart, what are you doing wringing your hands while that kitten suffers over there?

He stood mute, hand still on his chest.

— My sun, my star. Get your ass over there and deal with that kitten. And deadhead the daisies when you're done. I can't stand to see them looking so sad.

He bolted upright. His hip seized and a sharp pain shot down his leg. He steadied himself on the tree and took a deep breath. He smoothed his hair as he walked back over to the kitten.

She lifted her head slightly. He watched the fast rise and fall of her ribcage. A metallic smell when he bent to pick her up. She struggled at first but he held her close. He took her over to the house and sat down on the back porch. The steps were cold and splintery. He called to Clara and she came running over.

— Sylvia! Oh, my god. What happened?

The air smelled of dry grass. A bee buzzed in a lavender bush.

— I found her in a trap at the base of that tree.

She took the kitten in her arms.

— Why are there traps in your yard?

The man looked at her, his jaw tight. Leaves drifted silently around them. He heard the distant whirring of an airplane.

— I set them to catch the squirrels. It was an accident. I'm sorry.

She cuddled the kitten and started to cry.

— Oh, my god. Look at her. What's wrong with you?

He looked up. Sparrows flew like darts above them. The sky was a sheet pulled tight, the maple tree an orange cathedral rising into boundless blue.

— Leena?

He heard the faraway ding of a hammer. He stood up and dropped his cane onto the grass. Tears welled up and blinded him as he stumbled into the house.

Roadkill

★

BY CAM KING

CLUMP

The armadillos always jumped straight up when Screed's grimy red semi roared over their tiny little heads. Neither the angry hum of the tires, the rattling throb of the diesel, nor the blaring Big and Rich CD could totally mask the fatal clump that penetrated the dusty floorboard. The sound of impact was generally followed by a whoop of victory, a swig of Pearl, and a plug-stained grin from Screed. Perched behind the windshield of his old flat-faced Peterbilt, Screed watched the world split and fly past him as if it were a desert kaleidoscope. Delivering a load of Pecos Valley gas pipe and flying home, bug-spattered and Hell-bound for a cold one, Screed allowed his mind to escape the confines of the cab. He could feel the Texas asphalt flying beneath him as if he were walking inches above it in his bare feet.

Another humpbacked shadow on the road, this time in the oncoming lane. No traffic, no problem. Screed's three-fingered left hand easily pulled the power-assisted steering over just enough, bringing his screaming tires across the yellow line.

CLUMP

Wahoo!

And back again to the right. It was great to revel in the sure knowledge that he, Screed, had probably killed more armadillos than anyone in history.

It was a great day to be alive.

Screed took his name from his days as a concrete worker in Cincinnati. Finger-numbing Ohio winter wind and a little sleet never kept him from sloshing through freshly poured swales of Portland cement and rebar in knee-high rubber boots, a cement encrusted ten-foot pine 2x6 in his gloved paws. He knew enough Spanish to address the workers who grabbed each end of the heavy "screed" once he had laid it across the cold gray pudding. Working backward in a spine-warping crouch, they dragged, tapped, and herded the cement into a geometrically pure plane that Screed found profoundly satisfying, as if he were hewing a Newtonian order out of the wilderness. Romantic epithets like *andale, venga aqui, bueno, trabaja trabaja trabaja,* and *tu madre* were part of a gruff mantra that flowed from his lips as easily as the occasional amber jet of Red Man. He prided himself on his role of pathfinder in what he felt was a manifest malling of America. Then, on a gorgeous October morning, the front-end blade of a Bobcat intervened. His two left middle fingers, entombed in the slab of a Kentucky Walgreens, signaled the end of his empire-building days.

The fact that Screed's left hand was configured in a permanent "Hook 'em Horns" sign had nothing to do with his move three years ago to Brewhoe, Texas, a butt-ugly fistful of tin-roofed runes, cast among the dry cedar hills south of I-10 with no particular regard for order. Screed was done with Ohio Valley winters. He signed on with a trucking company that supplied steel gas pipe to the countless drilling rigs dotting the lower Pecos Valley. He was happy. His bosses didn't care if he drove the truck with his teeth. His single disability check became a down payment on a rocky half-acre of cedar and cholla, upon which sat a neoclassic Greek-styled mobile home. It was faced southwest, toward the land of those men whose gold-toothed smiles never wavered, even when Screed cursed them in two incomplete languages.

There was a single feature to Screed's aluminum and melamine Parthenon which worried the man who sold it to him, and vexed the crew who delivered it. Screed had himself built the concrete pad on which the home was to be mounted, complete with electrical and water hookups and septic, all presumably to code. However, the hillside it occupied was steep.

Very steep.

It ended four hundred feet below, not as level ground, but as a limestone precipice which towered another sixty feet above that section of County Road 17 known as Curvo Diablo. The engineers responsible for this blind curve felt that excessively banking the road slope to the inside would encourage thrill seekers to speed, so they banked and posted the curve for thirty-five miles an hour, on a highway otherwise designed for sixty-five. A bleached menagerie of plastic and aluminum memorial crosses decorating its shoulders gave mute testimony to their wisdom.

The driveway to the prepared slab was adequate for the delivery truck, since it looped around the crest of the hill, alleviating the need for any dangerous turnarounds. What bothered the people who saw Screed's home preparation was the fact that the slab itself was sloped more than a few degrees downhill. Screed had hurriedly slapped together a pier-and-beam foundation on bolts that were incorporated into the slab, and it was within this framework that he corrected and leveled the mounting base for the mobile home.

Seeing all this, the swarthy delivery driver grinned, *muy peligro*. Screed dismissed them all with an amber arc and a drowsy, laconic *no problemo*. He was not going to waste money on more base fill and footing volume than necessary. The slab was stable enough, and as far as he was concerned, its slope was an ingenious touch that would prevent standing water under his home.

Thus it was that the gleaming Navajo white hull with avocado trim was bolted down and hooked up on a Friday morning. It was keeping his weekend beer cold by that afternoon.

* * *

WELCOME TO HELL

The orange neon blinked again.

WELCOME TO HELL

Hell was the name of Screed's favorite bar; a name that belied the marketing genius of its owners. This was evidenced by their large displays of official T-shirts: GO TO HELL, I'M HELL BENT, SEE YOU IN HELL...the wearers of these sartorial statements were regularly expelled from public schools and admonished by traffic court judges to show more respect in their mode of dress.

The days of the jukebox were finished in Hell. Anybody looking for a comforting blanket of music to drape over their blues would now have to contend with four huge video monitors spewing oversaturated color images of nonstop NASCAR action. Broken hearts would no longer be nursed or mended by the Two Georges, Jones and Dickel, but by roaring nitro-fueled Pontiacs and Jello shots.

It was over such a plate of cinnamon schnapps and Stoli gel caps that Screed met the incredibly loud and unfailingly funny Shortblock. Shortblock was a self-proclaimed "mechanic to the stars" who wore his name in western font on the back of his forty-four-inch brown leather belt. There was no NASCAR event, either on live feed or videotape, on which he could not and would not weigh in personally, with all the gravity of a seasoned veteran.

Cain't hold with them queer-assed fire suits. Buncha growed up-babies in plastic pajamas, wanna wear they underwear on the outside like Superman.

Shortblock got the laughs, if not the girls—there were none to be had in Hell—and Screed did like to laugh.

* * *

CLUMP *Yay-yeah!!*
CLUMP *Gawd Dayam!!*

Screed and Shortblock were eastbound toward Ozona on I-10 when they got an unexpected bonanza. Armadillos were rarely found on the divided four-lane stretches of the interstate, partly because such wide paths of destruction effectively closed off any ancient migratory routes the little saurians once had, and partly because they had just plain been killed off. Yet, in little more than the space of a beer chug, under a rampart of towering August thunderheads, two large trophies had made their final startled ascents into Screed's oil pan. Shortblock saluted Screed with two fat upturned thumbs. The men had made the run out to Ft. Stockton the day before. Screed was delivering a load of pipe to a liquid petroleum gas distributor, and Shortblock was getting a reckless driving charge dismissed in exchange for his forgiving a betting debt.

The Ft. Stockton JP's son liked to gamble. On anything. Even NASCAR.

Shortblock liked to drive real fast at night. With his headlights off. Drunk.

Screed studied the dark eastern horizon, pocked with lightning. He looked back in his side mirror; the last of the sunburned trans-Pecos hills bounced away to the west.

The road was wet. The air was sticky and sweet with creosote bush. Screed was unaware of the latter; he and Shortblock were cocooned within a rolling, air-conditioned Skynyrd concert.

They musta been rained outa their burrows. Ain't seen this much summer rain since, hell, EVER.

Who the hell is they?

Them 'dillos. I usually get 'em at night. I put this thing up on two wheels once, just to get me one. Smeared his ass all over Highway 16 headed down to Kerrville.

Two wheels, my ass. You ain't had your short hairs stand on end 'till you slam down half a Cuervo and shoot down the middle of 290 with yer lights off, howlin' at the moon.

Shortblock, if you was any dumber, you'd be under my wheels ... What the—

CLUMP

This time there were no cheers.

Screed, was that 'dillo number three in as many miles?

Screed nodded, but squinted into his side mirrors. He hadn't really seen anything, just a shadow at the last second. It sounded heavier than usual. He turned up the CD player.

It truly had been a rainy summer for central Texas. The past seven years of drought had been flooded out by stalled fronts, thermal anomalies, and tropical storms thrown off course. All converged this year on the hill country. The creeks were full, the lakes were tight with surface tension, and right now the slick road was ready to toss a little hydroplane jujitsu at Screed's eighteen wheels. Screed would have none of that.

His eight fingers were better than most folks' ten, and he knew when to downshift, engine brake, and basically let dust collect on the brake pedal.

He was silent as they approached the exit to Brewhoe, which Shortblock assumed was due to Screed's concentration—lightning was cloud-to-ground all around them, and the wipers had already scraped off Screed's last application of Rain-X. The deluge was now collecting on the county road surface faster than it could run off. Screed's picture window view was like watching the parting of the Red Sea. A Kenworth tanker in front of them was plowing a pair of furrows in the water, and Screed was hugging dangerously close to take advantage of the relative traction offered by the tanker's tread paths.

As for his own silence, Screed had no lexicon from which to draw the words that would adequately describe his feelings, although *queasy* might have done for starters.

They neared the turnoff to Hell, where Shortblock had his cousin's 1996 Chevy Silverado dual-cab pickup parked. It was a platinum colored beast. It had a diesel engine exactly like the one which at that very moment was pulling them and eight tons of truck up the Edwards Plateau. It had a black deer guard across the grill, made of one-inch cold-rolled steel. Once, when Shortblock's cousin came home from a two-day bender, it had the head of an eight-point white tail buck wedged into its steel matrix.

Shortblock's own transportation, a rusting gray-primed 1978 Bonneville, had been on cinder blocks in his driveway for two weeks, waiting for him to get around to putting in a rebuilt water pump.

They pulled up to the front door of the bar.

Tell me it's midnight, Screed.

It's half-past three in the afternoon, can ya believe it?

Darker than a you-know-who's you-know-what out there. You up fer a round?

Naw, I'm getting' this thing parked and my ass up the hill before it gets any worse. Gonna be a six-pack and a box of movies for me tonight.

Shortblock held his canvas clothing bag over his head as he dove out of the cab and splashed the ten steps to the warm glow of Hell's front door. A phosphorescent blast of lightning—xenon and peach—lit up the parking lot somewhere close overhead. The flash and crack were instantaneous. Screed reached into his packet of Red Man, pushed a wad into his cheek, and drove out of the parking lot. It was another rainy mile down the highway to the pipe yard where his pickup was parked. He parked his rig under a truck shed and scrambled through the driving rain to get to his battered old brown Ford pickup. After two coughs and a goddamn, it fired up. With a symphony born of bad wiper blades and a perforated muffler, the F150 lurched forward and took off into the preternatural darkness.

A cloud-to-ground strike, really close. The street lights went off. Screed's headlight beams appeared to be sucked away into the darkness. He splashed on down Highway 17, anxious to reach the turnoff before Curvo Diablo and get up to his aerie on the black cedar lomita.

CLUMP

Holy shi—

CLUMP

Screed gagged as half a wad of Red Man tickled his uvula on its aborted journey south. He retched. It ended up not quite in his lap, not exactly on the dashboard.

This ain't EVEN funny no more. Damn little kamikazes...

The side road to Screed's hillside trailer was paved, and a slight break in the downpour allowed him to see where he was going. His driveway, however, was little more than a gravel aneurism which only got him within twenty feet of his front door. He could see that the power was on at his place; a tiny carriage light burned on each of the bas relief Corinthian columns which framed the front door. He dashed out through a renewed downpour, hit the hollow core door with the sound of keys, knees, and boot toes, and burst inside. The refrigerated air felt cold on his wet skin. He peeled off his wet T- shirt, toweled off, and put on a sleeveless one. He stepped into his bedroom and laid down in the dark.

CLUMP

Or was it thunder? It was a dream, maybe. Still dark. Had he slept? He looked at the glowing display of his bedside clock. 5:45. He walked to the refrigerator and opened it, blinking in the light as he pulled out a can of beer. Pop and a wet hiss. He paused in mid swallow, half turning toward the bedroom. Was that 5:45 PM or *AM*?

CLUMPCLUMP

Screed looked down at his feet. He had a strange feeling of motion, like being in a dream that was running away with him. He spread his feet a little wider, bent down with his right ear facing the floor.

CLUMPCLUMP CLUMP

Holy never-you-mind, I felt that!

He went to the front door. It was still raining, but it seemed less stormy. Lightning was silhouetting the hills to the south. Even with his porch lights on, Screed could barely make out the ground in front of him. He had planned to put in a lawn that winter, but right now it was mud, mud, mud. Or was it? He thought he saw something move. A possum. Or a skunk; hope not, knock on plywood.

Wait. Some *things* were moving. Through the drone of rain on metal and mud, he heard a scratching sound. It was familiar to him. Yes, the sounds of dozens of hermit crabs scratching around inside an empty beer crate.

Duh.

That was Key West, 1977.

What the hell....

He backed up a few paces, pulled open a kitchen drawer, and retrieved a black aluminum flashlight. He stepped out onto the front step and turned it on.

Screed's mind could accept something as bizarre as a family of raccoons sitting atop his garbage cans, munching away, and ignoring his shouts. But all he saw at first was a nonspecific movement, like brown waves on the surface of a dirty river by moonlight.

Right about the time the image in his mind clarified, confirming that what he saw was indeed a seething caldron of several hundred armadillos, Screed let out a childlike kind of half whoop. It sounded like *oops*. The armadillos didn't seem to respond to him, nor did they seem to be concerned with his presence. But they were busy. Some of them looked as if they were burrowing feverishly into fire ant mounds; others appeared to be coming out of the ground itself. That possibility was particularly disturbing, because it seemed that, even for the brief period he had been watching them, their numbers were increasing.

CLUMPCLUMPCLUMP

Screed leaned over the steps, pointed his flashlight through the white wooden latticework which skirted the base of the mobile home, and peered underneath.

They covered the hookup lines, the five-inch septic pipe, the diagonal boards, the beams where there was room. They were like zebra mussels on a spillgate; barnacles on a ship's keel. Armadillos in uncountable numbers were huddled in swarming, shapeless masses, scratching, rooting, bumping into each other and into the bottom of the mobile home.

CLUMPCLUMP

A flash of lightning, bright but silent, illuminated a human-like mask of horror only inches from Screed's face.

AAAAAAAAHHHH!!!!!

It was his reflection in the storm door glass. He swung the flashlight out at the boiling mass of wet chitinous armor. He would have to walk across them to get to his truck. His cell phone was out there; he had no land line. He dipped a foot out toward one armadillo. Six others reared up with a collective snort and clawed at his boot from every direction. He could feel the sharpness of their claws through the leather, and he pulled back. He looked at his boot. He could see the fibers of his red sock through a jagged tear. Wait, he was wearing white socks. He gasped and backed up into the doorway. Rivulets of rain trickled across his unblinking eyes; his breath came in quick, shallow pulses.

He backed into the middle of his living room/kitchen/den, leaving muddy prints on the ecru carpet. The scratching sound was everywhere. It came from below, from within the walls, even from the roof, ten inches above his head.

CLUMPCLUMPCLUMP

* * *

Shortblock woke up, his ponderous form stretched across the front seat of the hulking Silverado pickup. He sure tore Hell a new one tonight—he had been so excited to have cleared one bet the day before, only to come back to the bar and discover he had also won $500 on an easy call from the qualifying runs at Winston-Salem. Wanting to avoid a stormy drive home, he invented a game he called Thunder Chug, whose rules were simple and fairly obvious. When closing time came and went with no letup in the weather, he opted for the warmth and softness of the truck's leather seats, and drifted off almost immediately.

Now he was awake, sort of, and was aware of two things. No, three things. He wanted to get home, he wanted a beer and pizza, and he had to pee. Well, hold it. Number three was a simple case of number one, and the rain had eased to a point where he took care of that right then and there.

Now, since there was no beer and pizza at home, he knew he had to go six miles south of town on Highway 17, to the only all-night convenience store which featured those amenities. Maybe he'd wake up Screed on the way back and force him to join in. He turned the ignition key. Like an Apollo Saturn whose titanic engines are so far away they seem but a distant rumble to the astronauts strapped in their capsule, the sound of the Silverado's diesel reverberated from its lair, deep within the steel frame of the truck. Powerful and ominous, yet gentle... traveling in the soft cab of the Silverado was like riding on the back of a huge, tame grizzly. Shortblock swung the massive pickup in a wide drunken arc out of the parking lot and toward the southbound entrance to Highway 17. He flew up onto the wet asphalt without checking for traffic. He looked at the dash clock. It was ten minutes to six in the morning.

The road was empty in both directions. Shortblock couldn't believe his luck. He knew for a fact that state troopers and local law enforcement officers were almost never on this stretch of road at this hour. Distance and shift changes all figured in there somewhere, but those details were less important to him now than the opportunity to play his favorite game. Even though it was still dark outside, the lightning to the south flickered just enough to give him glimpses of the road ahead at varying intervals. He turned off his headlights, stepped on the gas, and howled like a coyote.

* * *

Screed was paralyzed. The flashlight in his hand pointed aimlessly toward the floor. He was dimly aware of a slight rocking, like those rolling earthquakes they had in California. Then the lights went out. He brought the flashlight beam back to the door in front of him, just in time to see, but not comprehend, the whole front of the trailer racing toward him.

Actually it was he racing toward it; the entire mobile home was pitching forward off its foundation. He felt a blissful moment of weightlessness, and then everything got loud and very painful. With a cacophonic splintering and metallic banging, the box in which Screed was now being slowly processed began to roll down the hill, ponderously at first, then gained speed with a momentum quite amazing for something so large. Water jetted upward from torn mains. Screed managed a moaning kind of scream as he was pinioned by something horribly heavy—a couch, perhaps—to the wall, which was already not a wall but a roiling bed of splinters and aluminum shards. He felt himself upside down, twisted like a doll with its limbs forced into wildly unnatural and excruciating position.

The rolling seemed to go on forever, but the smashing sound seemed to abate as the mobile home lost its rigidity and became more flexible as it was compressed.

Then, a moment of spinning silence.

Finally, a soul-shatteringly loud, single smash, some residual creaks and tinkles, and—nothing.

Screed lost not a single moment of consciousness during his terrible course down the hill, nor was he granted oblivion when the mobile home rolled off the limestone cliff and landed like a huge aluminum turd across both lanes of Curvo Diablo. He was, however, spared the agony of the ravages to his legs by the fact that his spine had been snapped at waist level. He moved his mouth noiselessly as he lay pinned inside the wreckage. The part of his brain that could observe these things as if from afar marveled at the silence of the night. Not a cricket chirped, not an owl hooted. But there was a snorting sound from somewhere above him, and—there was something else. A train? Not here. Growing louder. An angry sound, increasing in volume and pitch, according to the immutable laws of Doppler; its many overlapping echoes coalescing into a single banshee's shriek as it finally neared the welcoming arms of Curvo Diablo.

If Screed still possessed the neuromuscular facilities which would have afforded him the ability to smile, he would have done so. For the sound that came to his astral mind was the symphony by which he had lived, the music by which he had killed. It was the soundtrack to his life.

It was an 8.3-liter Cummins Diesel engine, singing at full throttle.

CLUMP

Tender 'Til the Day I Die

★

BY RHETT MILLER

"Won't you come away with me?"

He got the words out, but she was already twenty feet away. Out of earshot. Especially since he'd muttered the words under his breath. The kid reading a paperback in the Mystery/Thriller section heard him.

"She was pretty," the kid said.

"Still is. She's not dead." Joe pulled a slim volume from the box of books he'd bought off her on behalf of the Hey Penny Bookstore. The box radiated heat from having just been outside on the hot summer day. The cover of the pamphlet in his hand featured red type surrounding a black-and-white photo of John F. Kennedy on a stretcher, a sheet pulled back to expose the remaining half of his head. The box was filled with Kennedy stuff. The Warren Report. *A Life in Pictures*. Hard-core conspiracy tracts.

Joe didn't mean to snap at the kid. The kid was all right. Hung out every day reading till dusk. He'd work his way through an author's entire oeuvre before moving on. Now it was Ian Fleming's James Bond novels. Before that it had been Arthur

Conan Doyle. He asked the kid, "Do you think I'd have a shot? With her, I mean?"

The kid scrunched up his nose, considering the question. "You know I'm ten years old, right?"

Just then Ronald, the store's owner and Joe's uncle, slid through the propped-open emergency exit. "Am I paying to air-condition the street?" he demanded.

"Don't know. Doesn't seem to be working, does it?" Joe asked. He was stacking her books on the counter in front of him. As cool as he could, he smelled one to see if any of her lingered there. Nope. Just the smell of dust and old people. But he thought he could detect a trace of her scent on the warm cardboard box.

His brain pounded and his heart pumped. She was more beautiful than any other girl who had come into the store in the four years he'd worked there. Maybe she was a fashion model. He didn't get the feeling she was, though. Her hair stuck up, but like she'd slept on it, not like she'd put stuff in it. She excited Joe in a way that made him wish he led a fascinating life, that he had more ambition.

He knew she'd be back. She'd been coming in every few days for a couple of months, always with a stack of books to sell. Joe hadn't screwed up the courage to say anything to her. If this were a story in a book, she'd come back. And this time he would say it so she could hear him: "Won't you come away with me?"

The question had come to him last night while he drifted off to sleep. A car alarm went off somewhere down the street. As the honking persisted, these words came to Joe in the spaces in between: "Won't you come away with me?" It was the right question. And he meant it, too. He'd go. Not like to Venezuela to live forever, but maybe Hot Springs, Arkansas, or Nuevo Laredo. Hell, maybe Venezuela. Nothing to keep him here. Here was nowhere. Here was destined to be part of his past. Stacks of books stinking of old smoke. Dead readers. Dead pets. Dust. Mostly dust. He was a young man still.

Ronald put his big hand on Joe's shoulder and Joe jumped. Ronald had an ex-hippie ponytail but was built like a football player. "What'd you give her?"

"Twenty-six dollars," Joe answered.

"Jesus. Pretty fucking generous."

Joe pulled out some of the more yellowed and creepy-looking items and explained, "I thought these might fetch a pretty good price on eBay."

Ronald grunted. "Just 'cause she gives you a boner doesn't mean I should go broke."

When Joe got home, his roommate Fred was on the computer.

"Jack's Burger House burgers are in the oven keeping warm," Fred called out. Burgers were all he ate. Cheeseburgers. "Fries, too." And french fries. He was a connoisseur of these items, encyclopedic in his knowledge of the city's hamburger/ french fry selection.

"Cool. Thanks for waiting."

They ate cheeseburgers and smoked pot out of a bong. A hockey game played on the television. Joe listened to Fred complain about how one of his two girlfriends had been at the house all afternoon crying. She thought Fred paid too much attention to the other girlfriend.

"I don't even know if it's worth it anymore. I mean the sex is awesome, obviously, but two chicks, man? With two chicks worth of problems? All the time?" Fred talked with his mouth full. "But the sex is bad-ass. I mean, half the time I don't have to do anything except kick back and watch."

"I know," Joe said. "My bedroom wall is a tarp, remember?"

Not exactly an engineering masterpiece, Joe's bedroom wall was a ten-by-fifteen- foot sheet of paint-speckled plastic stapled to the ceiling. He cut a slit down the middle for a door. The tarp converted what had been the downstairs/living room portion of the garage apartment into a semi-private environment. Joe constantly reminded himself that this was a temporary setup and his life would evolve into something better. That this was his cocoon and that he would emerge, butterfly-like, someday.

That night, both of Fred's girlfriends came over. Apparently they made up.

Part Two

Joe propped open the emergency exit to generate a breeze through the store. He was reading a book about Ireland. The book described the Irish Sea as lonely. Joe liked that. He thought about taking up cigarettes in order to kill off some of his olfactory powers. The smell of old books was so specific and affecting. Joe could hardly inhale without experiencing claustrophobia. He wondered if he was going crazy, going under.

"Won't you come unbury me?" he whispered to himself. He tried to determine the provenance of this line and remembered repeating it to himself as he drifted off to sleep the night before.

This time the ten-year-old bibliophile in the mystery/thriller section didn't hear him, but someone Up There must have, for the front door opened and she walked toward him with a paper grocery sack clutched to her chest. She set it down on the counter and stared at him for a moment. He remembered the old *Laverne & Shirley* gag where Carmine or Frank DeFazio would say something along the lines of, "Only an idiot would go out in weather like this." And Lenny and Squiggy would burst in, all leather and pomade, and Squiggy would call out, "Hello" in a pinched, nasal punchline of a voice. Joe had asked the universe for rescuing and... "Hello."

He stared back at her. Her hair wasn't sticking up as chaotically as it had the day before. She'd put barrettes in it to keep it off her forehead. She had little freckles on her face that reminded Joe of sparse constellations. Her hands, resting on the rolled top of the grocery sack, were pale with long tapered fingers. Joe remembered reading somewhere that tapered fingers signified royal lineage. Her nose was maybe a little too big for her face. He wanted to kiss its bridge and feel her cheekbone resting in his eye socket.

She started to say something, reconsidered, and pushed the bag towards him. Joe unrolled the top and removed a stack of Travis McGee paperbacks by John D. MacDonald.

"These are great," Joe told her, meaning it. "I love how Travis McGee lives on a houseboat."

"I know. Slip F-18, Bahia Mar. I read them all." She picked up *A Purple Place For Dying* and opened it to the title page. "They're autographed."

"Wow."

"Yeah. My grandmother was obsessed with him. She tracked him down in the eighties before he died."

"Why are you selling them? Never mind. That's rude."

"That's okay. She doesn't want them anymore." Her strength ebbed. Her fingers wound into each other and her eyes welled up and fell down toward the books. "Fuck," she whispered. "I'm such an asshole."

Her shoulders heaved. She let loose a small wail and suddenly she was crying. The 10-year-old kid edged down the aisle and disappeared around an end-cap. Instinctively, Joe reached over the counter and took her hand. It was warm. Her long fingers squeezed him.

"Hey, it's all right. It's gonna be all right." He lowered his face into her line of vision and made eye contact with her. She laughed once through her tears and said, "I'm sorry. You're right. I haven't slept at all. I've been up all night for weeks reading my grandmother's books." She straightened as if remembering something, pulled her hand from Joe's, wiped the tears from her freckled cheeks, and asked, "So, can you buy these?"

Joe winced. "Yeah, I mean, sure. The thing is, these are actually worth some money and I can't really do it until my boss shows up. And, frankly, he's a dick. He's not gonna give you even close to what they're worth. You should sell them yourself on eBay. You'd get a lot more."

"Yeah... I don't have a computer. I'm not good at all that stuff."

"I could help you." Joe realized that maybe he seemed creepy. He wiped his forehead with his sleeve and said, "Look, you seem nice. If you want, we could meet up at the library or an Internet coffee shop or something and I could show you how to do it. Sell stuff on the Internet."

"How long would it take?"

"Just an hour or so."

"No, I mean the turnaround on selling them on the Internet."

"Gosh. A couple of weeks."

The slamming of the emergency exit door startled Joe. He wheeled around to see Ronald. His boss had apparently overheard a significant portion of the exchange because he was charging toward the sales counter. He looked pissed.

"Joe, you and I are going to have a serious talk," Ronald said. He turned to address the customer. "I'm sorry, ma'am. How can I help you?"

She looked from Ronald to Joe and stammered something incomprehensible.

Ronald pulled a book from her bag, opened it to the title page, and said, "Autographed? Nice. I'd be willing to give you, say, seven dollars a book."

Joe snorted.

She scrunched up her face and said, "You know what? I can't sell these. Not right now anyway." She put the books back in the bag.

The way the afternoon sunlight concentrates itself on her right cheek, Joe thought, it must be in love with her as well.

Joe said, "Ronald, you're a dick."

Ronald said, "Joe, you're fired."

"Gosh, Uncle Ronnie, that's too bad. That means you're going to have to pay my unemployment."

On his way to the front door, Joe called out to the ten-year-old kid lurking in the corner, "Get outside and soak up a little sunshine. It's only a matter of time before we all croak, right?"

Next to Joe, the girl pulled a paperback out of her grocery sack and tossed it to the kid. His eyes grew wide and he hollered thank you as Joe and the girl breezed out of the Hey Penny Bookstore.

Part Three

Joe offered to carry her bag of books. They walked slowly past the shops of the strip mall. Joe could feel her eyes on him.

"Regarding the question you asked as I was leaving the other day: Where did you have in mind?" she asked.

"Excuse me?" Joe needed a second to process this.

"Won't you come away with me?' I have excellent hearing. Ever since I had an ear infection when I was seven. It's not always such a great thing. I can hear couples fighting in adjacent houses."

"Oh. So you heard me?"

"You were talking to me, right?"

"I'm a mess."

She laughed. "So, where did you have in mind?"

They walked to the park. She told Joe that her name was Anna. They laid down on the grass and held hands.

"Nagy-mama isn't nagy-mama anymore." she said, pronouncing it so that "Nagy" sounded like "nyugh."

"Is that what you call your grandma?"

"It's Hungarian for grandmother. She came over here when she was about my age. Fleeing the Communists. She went from the aristocracy to a tomato-canning factory in the blink of an eye. She never got bitter about it. Her husband did, but she didn't."

"You loved her a lot."

"I still do."

"Where is she?"

"Sunnydale Retirement Community. It's a fucking morgue is what it is. She's got Alzheimer's. A couple of months ago, they found her wandering around by Fair Park. She'd walked so far that her feet were bloody and she didn't know where she was. Or who she was, really."

"Ouch." They were quiet a little while.

Anna cried again, big tears this time. Joe kissed them away as they rolled down over her freckles.

The sun set over the humming electrical relay station. Anna didn't have a car, so Joe gave her a ride to Nagy-mama's house. Anna moved in when they put Nagy-mama in the old-folks' home. The house was a small, red brick affair surrounded by huge, new, zero-clearance-lot behemoths. Joe pulled his car into the driveway in the shade of a pine tree that sprawled the width of the front yard. Joe thought the tree must have been three hundred years old.

The house was spare and grandmotherly. Bookshelves lined the walls. They were mostly full, but Joe could tell that significant chunks had been removed. Anna explained that she had been selling off her grandmother's collection.

"She won't ever be able to read again. My parents don't care. I feel bad about it, but I don't have an income. I made a deal with myself that I wouldn't sell any of her books until I'd read them." Anna made a face at Joe. "I know that's crazy, but I felt like it was important."

There was a globe on an end table. Joe spun it and said, "Wherever my finger lands is where I'm gonna move." Anna laughed. Joe squeezed his eyes shut and put his finger down. "Prague." He let his finger slide off the globe and fall with a thud on the table. "Who am I kidding?" Joe said. "I've got inertia like a fucking disease." This made Anna laugh.

She made chili while he put together a salad. They ate on the back porch next to a garage that leaned at a forty-degree angle.

"Basically, my mom and dad are just waiting for her to die. They've got a realtor who's already got a buyer lined up. The buyer's hired an architect who's drawn up plans. This house will be razed a week after she dies, which won't be long now."

"You don't think she could hang on for a while?"

Anna shook her head. "There are all sorts of complications, issues, medical bullshit. Do you know what usually happens with Alzheimer's people? They get starved to death. How fucked is that?" Anna shook her head and smiled at Joe. "I'm sorry. I'm not much of a first date, am I?"

"I like how sad you get. I feel like a fucking zombie myself half the time."

She kissed him then.

They spent the night in a creaky old bed in a house that wouldn't be there next spring. They kept their clothes on, but when they woke, they were wrapped up in each other. Bound together by need and design.

Part Four

The next day, they drove to the Sunnydale Retirement Community. On the way, Anna told him how Nagy-mama was convinced that her Alzheimer's was the result of extended exposure to the rubber cement she'd used every day as secretary to the president of a savings and loan.

"It wasn't even like she was gluing industrial-grade shit," Anna said. "It was slips of paper into a book. The boss just made her use rubber cement for some reason."

The Alzheimer's wing smelled like crisis, Joe thought, an urgent smell of everything going wrong. The nurses seemed to be hiding. Nagy-mama woke up when they entered her room. She smiled and blinked.

A woman's voice called through the curtain, "You better not be having another party, you. Always with the noise and the parties, you."

Nagy-mama's watery eyes settled on Anna then softened with vague recognition. "Oh, it's you, honey." Her voice, barely a whisper, sweetened the air in the room. Anna gave her grandmother's cheek a gentle kiss.

Nagy-mama noticed Joe and squinted. "Travis McGee," she said, which made Joe crack up.

"I wish," he said.

"Nagy-mama, this is Joe. He's my boyfriend." Anna reached out and touched Joe's shoulder. Nagy-mama started to say something, but couldn't make the words. Anna spoke instead. "I brought you a present." Anna reached into her large purse and extracted a plastic sandwich bag containing a pinecone covered with bird seed. "It's from the tree in your front yard. I put some peanut butter in it and rolled it in bird seed just like you taught me when I was little."

She smiled at Nagy-mama and handed her the gift. "I thought we could hang it outside your window and you could watch the birds."

Nagy-mama took it and squeezed it. It made a slight crunch. "Bird? Butter?" She looked at Anna, lost.

The woman on the other side of the curtain called out, "Lights out time. Party's over time."

For the third time in two days, tears flowed down Anna's freckled cheeks. "I love you so much, Nagy-mama. This isn't fair. This is not how it's supposed to be."

As Nagy-mama reached out and squeezed Anna's forearm, a stern look came across her features. "Stop crying. You need to pull yourself together. I am not dead, girl. Stop crying."

Anna appeared to almost smile. She hiccuped and let a sharp breath escape her lips. "I'm sorry. You're right. What was I thinking?" She turned to Joe. "Would you mind waiting down by the car? I think we need a minute alone is all."

"Certainly."

Part Five

A few nurses loitered on the edge of the parking lot, smoking. Joe thought about asking them for a cigarette, thought again about taking up smoking. Probably one of them had a flask. He could have used a taste of something. He sat on the trunk of his car, turned his face up to the sky, and thought about how quickly things change.

Joe used his cellphone to call his mom. When she answered, he immediately regretted having called. He could hear his father in the background yelling something about Uncle Ronald and respect. Joe told his mom that that everything was falling apart, but in a good way. He didn't expect her to understand, but he asked her to trust him. Joe's father grabbed the phone and said, "You know what I call this, Joe? Pilot error, Joe."

"Guess what, Dad"—Joe tried to keep his voice calm —"I'm stepping on the gas and letting go of the wheel. How do you like them apples?" Joe snapped his phone shut. He had rehearsed this speech a million times in his mind. Spoken aloud, it sounded stilted and immature. Joe felt profound disappointment.

A white shuttle bus pulled into the parking lot. The double doors lurched open and a big, mustachioed man in scrubs appeared in the doorway. Before climbing out, he turned back to face the passengers, who appeared to be residents of the Sunnydale R.C. He called out, "Y'all stay here. I gotta go take a leak. I'll be right back." He sprinted in through the automatic front doors of the facility.

Joe watched the old folks sit and fidget. Then, suddenly, one of them headed for the open front door. The little old man wore a fedora and moved slowly, holding onto the headrests of the seats he passed. He reached the front and moved sideways down the first big step, holding the railing. Joe watched as seven or eight fellow passengers followed suit, standing and hobbling down the center aisle. As the first old man reached the bottom step, he lost his grip and went headfirst to the pavement. Joe rushed over to help.

The smoking nurses had disappeared.

The old man blinked and moaned as Joe arrived. A small patch of blood on the old man's temple made his stomach turn. An old woman stepped off the bus and all her weight landed on the injured man's left shin. He cried out. Joe caught the old woman just before she collapsed on top of the old man. She whimpered in Joe's arms as he laid her on the pavement. The others kept coming.

"Wait, wait," Joe cried. He stood and tried to block the bus's doorway.

As he held the doorframe and tried to stem the tide, he heard Anna's voice call his name from somewhere up above. He looked over his shoulder and there she was, tying the pinecone to the tree branch outside Nagy-mama's window.

The mustachioed nurse ran up and surveyed the scene. He got right in Joe's face. "What the hell are you doing?"

"Your job, dick."

The nurse put his hand on Joe's shoulder. This was weirdly soothing for a moment, but then it caused Joe to lose his grip. A small gang of old people fell out of the bus and landed on top of Joe and the nurse. Lying in the middle of this pile of humanity, Joe looked up and saw Anna waving and smiling at him.

Baby Doll

★

BY PATTY LARKIN

Baby Doll was no baby. That went without saying. Who would argue that the sixty-three-year-old somewhat garrulous woman was childlike? Or that she was much of a looker, to be perfectly frank. But, somehow, the name had stuck. When you're two years old you own the world, and the world claims you the best it can. Red haired and freckle faced, Baby Doll had won the hearts of her three older brothers who adored her, at first, treating her like a China doll; then they put her back in the box from puberty on up. So, you see, it was Baby Doll one way or another.

She was from Covington, Kentucky—a place on the flipside of the tracks on the wrong side of the river. To this day Covington has been slow to pick up. The Hooters moved in down by the levee, but it still only has one Starbucks. Across the Ohio River stood Cincinnati plain as day for all to see. Covington's answer to that was gambling, cheap liquor, and prostitutes. Yes, indeed. Right there on the buckle of the Bible Belt. It was hard to praise the Lord and make a living, so Baby Doll's family had slowly settled itself into the seamier side of things.

Her grandfather was the proprietor of a speakeasy back when they were a necessary evil. So it stood to reason that her father would follow in grandpa's footsteps. He owned a liquor store within spitting distance of the bridges. "Easy Access," he had called it. When the war came Baby Doll's brothers were drafted in and one of them moved East to grease the axles of the planes flying off Cape Cod. Baby Doll had seen postcards of the place thumbtacked to her neighbor's garage wall, the hand-painted three by fives of cottages with pink roses at the gates, of lighthouses with lobsters and seagulls painted in the corners with GREETINGS FROM CAPE COD written on a diagonal across the scene. She had wondered at somewhere so different from the brick row houses, the factories and the mills, so much so that having just turned the corner on eighteen, she decided to keep going and leave town. One small bag and a long train ride later, she stepped out into the June sun to a place she had never been, people she had never known, and decided it was all a big mistake.

Just the same, she had her brother, and there was no turning back now. On his days on leave, her brother and his friends drove with Baby Doll down to the tip of the Cape to see what was there. Sand mostly. Truro didn't make her feel any better. The place was perched on a godforsaken cliff above the Atlantic. Where tourists saw a photo op, Baby Doll only saw what she thought were German submarines. The fact that they were whales heading north to feed didn't change her mind much. This was a dangerous, faraway place with odd-talking people. Still and all, she got a job cleaning the toilets of the wealthy folks in Centerville, lived in town as far from the surf as possible in a rented room above the hardware store, and bit by bit she got used to the idea of planting roots in the sandy soil.

Toward the end of the war she met Samuel Cole, a mechanic from the Lower Cape who worked with her brother and, after six months of days thinking only about him and her together, they got married. He was a boy in a man's body, drove a car that was new once, too. He had grown up on the Cape, called it "the sand spit," and had little or no desire to cross the bridge to whatever lay beyond. They moved to the Outer Cape, where it narrowed down to nothing. Up in Maine they would have called Baby Doll "From Away." Out there she was a "Wash Ashore." Fine by Baby Doll. That's exactly how she felt.

And so, she stayed. They moved beyond the flex of the Cape's arm and made a life for themselves. She and Sam lived in a ranch house in Wellfleet with a garage right next door. Not a car garage, but a repair place. Sam imagined himself a knower of all things automotive, but in reality the wealth of his knowledge ended with the Dodge Dart. The late '80s found him mechanically stumped. Luckily, there were enough old cars around town, shuffling down Route 6 and bumping down the sand roads in the woods, that he kept himself busy. Sam fixed what he could and what he couldn't ended up in the backyard for spare parts. Baby Doll had her own idiosyncrasies. The woman had never met a lawn ornament she didn't like. Two mirror balls, a doe with its fawn in tow, three rabbits, one butt-in-the-air gardener with polka dot bloomers, a windmill, a goldfish pond, and two leprechauns adorned her small patch of lawn. It got worse around Christmas when everything was lit up with big colored bulbs, including a Santa, reindeer, a blowup snowman, and a manger. She called everyone Honey, so the summer people called her Honey, too. Not to her face, so much as in reference to. Her hair was box red, her lipstick the same, and, like Sam, her fashion sense had ended in 1967. Funny how people get stuck in their favorite decade. She worked at the diner on Main Street, the Sand Dune, serving locals year-round, and tourists from shoulder season to shoulder season. That's where she was the day Hurricane Bob rolled into town.

The day had started much like the one before. Out on the back shore dawn came up in a thin red line below clouds that hung like a curtain of dark purple. The tide went out and you could tell it all over town. Baby Doll was up at five with enough light to make coffee and get to work. By eleven her brother called from Florida: "Have you filled the tub yet?" All that way up the coast and you could still hear the Kentucky in his voice. "What are you talkin' about?" Baby Doll shot back, rolling her eyes. One thing she could still do is stand up to her brothers. "The hurricane, for Chrissakes. It's headed right to your door!" She hadn't been following the storm even though she had heard the regulars waxing poetic about it all morning, but wasn't that the case with fishermen to talk about bad weather. She put down the phone, looked at the blank face in the corner of the restaurant, walked over, and turned it on. Maps and arrows screamed across the screen, then the screen switched to a reporter standing in front of crashing waves, then back to the map and arrows. There it was, clear as a bell, the huge yellow arrow with the hurricane swirl attached was cutting across the ocean and aimed right for the heart of Wellfleet! Panic stuck in her throat, her heart quickened, she ran back to the phone. "It's headed here! They never make landfall, though. Don't you think it'll blow right out of steam?" Her eyes bulged and she searched the ceiling. "Fill the tub," he said in a monotone.

Baby Doll hung up her apron, turned to the manager and told him she had to "scoot." "Be back in a half," he said. Out on the street you could feel the change in the air. Something seemed charged, and the light was, well, strange. "Shit," she said out loud. People were looking a little strange, too. They were rushing out of the market with jugs of water, bags of bread, bottles of liquor. The essentials. She hurried home and switched on the TV, went and filled the tub. If they lost power, they lost water; if they lost water, no toilet. She and Sam had been meaning to get a cheap generator for just this occasion, but shoulda, woulda, coulda. Outside the wind was picking up. Her new little weather vane was spinning around in circles. The fawn was already blown down and the mirror balls were reflecting trees that were starting to sway. Sam came running up the walk with a bottle of bourbon. "Whoa!" he said as he slammed the door. They filled the lobster pot with clean drinking water, made coffee, and sat in front of the newscaster up until the first pine tree snapped into two. "It's here!" they both said at the same time. Things were happening fast now. The sky grew dark with rain, and the wind really kicked in. One by one trees broke at the waist like some aerobics class gone wrong. "Let's get away from these windows," said Sam with an odd twist in his voice.

They left the living room picture window on its own just as a full force hurricane bore down. They grabbed the one good flashlight and headed for the unfinished basement. Unfinished is a kind way to put it. Uninhabitable was more like it. They sat on the cold, damp cement under the bare twenty-five-watt bulb and began to wait. Outside the wind was roaring. They could hear the crash of more trees coming down, of breaking glass as the mirror balls smashed on the asphalt drive. "Merry Christmas," Baby Doll said under her breath. Then, "God bless us and save us!" as things went from bad to worse. She was really scared now and Sam knew it. He was not having much fun either, but he'd been through this before as a teenager when a hurricane in the '30s carried the ocean water a mile inland. This was just something to ride out. He began to hum softly into Baby Doll's ear, his breath warm with coffee. Up close he could smell the shampoo in her red curls, the grease from a morning's worth of fried potatoes, and a salty not altogether unattractive sweat. He hummed an old song, one from their stand around the piano days. Slowly he started to sing, "In a shady dell, by a mountain stream, dwells sweet Nora Shannon, she is Nature's queen." The words came out slow and low, interrupted by a crash here, a bump there. He went on, "Bright as the sunshine," craaaack, "she is the girl I adore," whoosh, "each day I see her, I love her more…" Just then the bulb above their heads went brown once, twice, and on the third time the electric power all across Cape Cod blinked and went out. "Oh shoot," Sam said. "Our goose is cooked." Baby Doll had to agree. They sat still in the dark basement.

Out on Bound Brook, locust trees were falling like toy soldiers. The oak and pine were coming down, too, blocking the sand road that ran off Old County. It would be ten days before the power came back out there. With no phone and the power out it took all of the next morning for a kind soul from town and his son to chainsaw their way down the road tree by tree and check on the eighty-year-olds who lived out there on what used to be an island.

Meanwhile in Baby Doll's basement something else happened. She and Sam began to sing. Little bits of things at first. She started in with "Boogie Woogie Bugle Boy" in more of a frog's voice than anything else. "Doodleyadda doodleyadda, doot doot, doot, eight to the bar," she croaked. Sam laughed softly. He sang "Rhapsody in the Rain" like a chicken and that made her laugh, too. She stopped worrying about what was happening outside. He sang a pretty darned good version of "Itsy Bitsy Teeny Weenie Yellow Polka Dot Bikini." "You wish," was all Baby Doll said as she looked him in the eye and winked. Things just took off from there. All those years of working with the oldies station on in the background must have sunk in somewhere. They sang songs from the '50s, songs from the '70s, songs they loved and ones they never knew they knew. They played it up on the chorus of "Windy." They did show tunes. They sang Pat Boone and Sinatra, Doris Day and Dinah Shore. Mwah! They blew kisses at each other.

When it came time to finally crawl out of the basement, they came up for air and took a look at the mess from their living room window. The sight just brought up the Beatles. "Help!"

they sang at the top of their lungs. With night coming on they gathered up a few candles, searched the house for old batteries, and made dinner on the propane stove before it got too dark to see. They were out of power for the next seven days. With no TV and no radio to pass the time, they spent the long evenings singing. They sang gospel songs and folk songs, Tin Pan Alley songs, and the "contemporary hits." They sang songs of love lost and found, songs of fires and storms, ships and women, women and home, women and drinking, cheating women, cheating hearts, Jesus, babies, lost babies, home, going home, never going home, growing old, and death. They sang a Gordon Lightfoot album in its entirety, starting with "If You Could Read My Mind." They did Willie and Woody, Dylan and Baez, Patsy, Johnny, and Elvis in one long medley.

Friday night they moved to their back patio, and the neighbors came by and joined in. Now there were even more songs to sing. One of them went and got his guitar, and Ruby Silva went home and took a round-backed mandolin off the wall, came back, and started strumming. Life returned as normal as it got once the lights came back on. Even so, things would never be quite the same. After Hurricane Bob some light went on in Sam and Baby's head that couldn't be turned off. They started a sing every Friday night at their house, and when the weather turned cold they moved it all indoors and kept going. Winter came, and they moved their sessions out the door to the church basement. They got invited to sing at the Legion Hall and for a couple of parties, a church social here or there. It got so that it was just the four of them: Sam and Baby Doll, Ruby and the guitar player, Xavier. They called themselves The Hurricanes. When the first Wellfleet Oysterfest happened the committee asked them to sing on the main stage behind town hall. Things took off from there. They played opening night at the Provincetown Film Festival where they met John Waters who was so taken, he put them in his next movie. They became an underground sensation. Seemed that their fashion sense put them smack dab in the middle of hip. All this was beyond Baby Doll. She kept driving her 1979 black Buick sedan right into the next century. She coasted through town like a slow boat. Baby and Sam were slowing down themselves. They cut down on all the hoopla, the travel gigs and whatnot, and went back to sitting in their living room singing for themselves. They knew more songs than they could sing in a month. Some new, some old, all the ones that washed ashore the day that Hurricane Bob blew through town. Some melodies come and go. This one stayed on forever.

from:
Afterimage
★
BY DAMON KRUKOWSKI

How quickly the tales we tell ourselves and each other, the small rationalizations, the hopes and excuses, even the snatches of songs and poems, build in our lives not to a crescendo, but into a wall that blocks the view. We sit as in a garden, the walls protect and define the space, but whether we turn to one another or inward to peer at ourselves, these calcified stories impinge our movements, our heads and hips no longer swivel freely. And then one day some bit of story breaks loose, swirls through the body like a fish finally past a dam, lodges in a small crevice of the heart or mind, and brings the novel to an end.

These were my thoughts a few days following a conversation in which it seemed nothing that wanted to be expressed, could be. Or rather nothing that was expressed, was received as such. All sides were left wanting.

The landscape slipped by the train. I felt like that bit of story, hurtling toward and then into the most intimate parts of the city.

That evening, in the dark, my friends played music to a room of strangers. They sang,

> *I am riding, I am riding*
> *Forthcoming from the inside*

And I was struck by their reversal of the image I had earlier conceived: my friends' feelings, from the inside, were exploding outward toward the crowd. Using the story's own force, they have parried its thrust, and put its power to use. The story is a dynamo.

*

The next morning, I finally give my parents a copy of my book of poems. These poems are the destructive bits of story in my life, swept together like crumbs. In the first one, my father builds a wall, but underground:

> *Eventually we covered the trench over, and said a prayer*

I cannot watch their reaction. I give them the book and immediately leave.

*

In Seoul, Korea, the rain has stopped, we are walking with our hosts after dinner. The small square in the center of this neighborhood is filled with young people cooking on bunsen burners, playing badminton, drinking beer. The makkoli seller arrives, pushing a gigantic cart stacked with white bottles. "Sake?" I say to B. "Or milk?" he suggests. The makkoli seller spots B., six feet tall, stops his cart and strides up to him. The makkoli seller is equally tall. He addresses B. in a few words of broken Japanese

—"Delicious! Healthy!"—and then something in Korean that makes the women in our group laugh. The men are pushing us away. "Taste it! Korean rice wine," he explains, this time in English. B. shakes his head no. The makkoli seller pours the white liquid into a paper cup, eyes locked with ours. Still smiling, he pours it on the ground.

※

The temptation to write a little each day—the invitation, the promise, the imperative—has often presented itself. Just a little, and by the end of a year imagine how much writing you will have done. But why write so much? Why add to the endless march of days, recorded or not? Why not one page per year; or better yet, one per lifetime. But why that too. Why any page at all. Why add. What wisdom it would be, not to write.

*

Lisbon, some months prior to Korea: walking in the dawn because the bed was too uncomfortable for sleep. Bakeries unlocking their gates. Streets wet, whether from rain or from having been washed I do not know. Wandering, but taking care not to get lost—tracing the route seen from above, as on a map. I stumble on Pessoa's favorite café, pointed out the day before. A coffee at the bar: *"O melhor café é o d'A Brasileira."*

I realize I have not been wandering. This back and forth across the map—does it not trace a familiar route? There is no war; on the contrary, our travels for music depend on peace, predictability—Spain and Portugal were only added to the itinerary once the Fascists were truly gone. But the refugee's path is likewise an opportunistic zig-zag. Looking for asylum. Longing for a coffee at the bar.

The city awakening. Morning sounds of no fear.

*

Chronology is another temptation, another trap. Why write each day; why write in order of the days. These are middle-class ideals of efficiency, productivity.

*

The medicine show arrives, and we unpack its carefully collapsed props from a set of nesting crates. All is arranged for transport foremost, maximum effect second. A red top hat packs flat as the plates in the moveable kitchen. A headdress of ostrich feathers is revealed, on closer inspection, to be painted silk and tin. Every material dissembles; even many of the foodstuffs are ersatz, whether for economy, longevity, stage use, or all three. These jars of beans might be stones. A bread, one slice removed, is in fact paper and paste. This ham is made of wood; but the bacon, equally hard, smells sweetly of smoke. Ambiguity protects the goods from pilfering—who can be sure which hammer bends like rubber, which chair collapses at the slightest pressure, which pot is filled with grease paint and which with cooking fat?

*

Another city with its face smeared in burnt cork. Its noises might be anywhere near the sea: Barcelona, San Francisco, Taipei. A resident would recognize the idle of domestic cars, the type of warning whistle one can ignore. But the visitor falls for them all, without question, without guile. The visitor is an audience.

Once the visitor starts a routine, the city becomes the audience. This is why the performer carries a city with him, packed in crates.

*

How to cut through the routine of received ideas, habits of thought—cut through like a train through the city. Look to the backs of houses, disused lots, community gardens, concrete river-beds. Don't look to faces—faces are smeared in burnt cork.

*

We rehearsed in the garden. It was midday, too hot to be out-side. Behind us, two men work to erect a backdrop painted with characters—"wind" and "sound"—but the frame they have built is unsteady, it keeps falling over. We feel the heat on our instruments.

*

Go ahead and mention the book you are writing, like Ovid's writings in exile—he describes the situation of the book, and writes the book, without any disjuncture. Both are the truth. The truth of the situation, and the artificiality of it. The wander-ing, and the route it traces.

*

I should mention the book I have already written, as well: a book of poems. These poems are the destructive bits of story in my life, swept together like crumbs. In the first one, my father builds a wall, but underground:

> *Eventually we covered the trench over, and said a prayer*

A few months after this was published, my aunt E.—my father's only sibling—died. The day of the funeral, after we had watched her casket lowered into the ground, my father said to me: "It reminded me of your poem, about the time I hid in the root cellar." I was confused. Which poem? "The one about the time I hid in the ground and didn't come out for three days—you know the story." (I did not.) "When L. left." (His nanny, sent away when the war started.) "The smell of the earth—it always makes me think of it."

That day he also said: "There's no one left, no one who was there."

*

Clue to the power of silent movies: Clara Bow's career was ruined when sound revealed her heavy Brooklyn accent. This accent undoubtedly helped her silent performances, however.

*

We crossed Spain, and crossed it again. Cities rose up out of the plain, and fell back again into nothing. We crossed Spain, littered with the memory of cities.

We drive into the center of one, Valladolid. Everyone in the city has forgotten everything—this is because the Fascists had been there, and no one wants to remember them.

How do you sing to an audience with no memory? We try to sing songs like those cities on the plain—rising up out of nowhere, and disappearing just as quickly. Why add to these people's memories, if they want none.

Singing like this feels like singing into a heavy black void.

The sax player upends a bottle of water into his horn. A watery solo follows: bubbles of air emerge from the mouthpiece, and float up to the ceiling.

I realize I have described this experience, some years before. It was a poem written in the second person, perhaps because I had not yet myself lived it. It is a memory written in advance of experience. Does that make it a song for Valladolid? I will retitle it now:

Valladolid

Experience of singing is for you an auditory one, you have never sung aloud. You cannot remember doing so, at least. Singing while asleep is possible, even beautiful, the pitch is perfect and breathing effortless. Nevertheless no sound emerges during such performances. The breath you exhale is suspended, little bubbles escape as from a swimmer but there is no room for air, the space inside is completely full with nothing, and motionless. When you wake, breathing is normal but awkward. Your throat is scratchy as if from yelling. Glycerin is useful in lubricating your unused vocal cords. You have been under water a long time.

* * *

Crawl

★

BY ROBBIE FULKS

Slouched forward, chin sunk heavily in hand, David Semple screwed his face into a mental-gears-grinding shape and gazed over his nameplate, past the tiered seats and the forty strangers before him, and out the broad windows of Hamilton Hall. Twilight was moving in. Several dozen young men and women lay in loose pairs, scattered across the soft lawn, absorbed in earnest study, as others with backpacks and bottles of brand-name water intersected the rectangle in purposeful straight lines from all points. On the steps of John Jay opposite Hamilton, a few pigeons dawdled. Overhead, the windows of the dorm rooms —hard to imagine, one of them had cradled the ravening embryo of John Berryman—sat placid and dim.

David hadn't been back to the city in twelve years, to the college in nineteen, and he was starting to wonder if he was emotionally prepared for the twin re-encounters. His brain, unlike the orderly students on the lawn, was spraying in all directions, like a loose showerhead. "Ginsberg...Holly Woodlawn...Abe Beame...giant rats...Lone Star (Too Much Ain't Enough!)...Furnald Hall...Hapsburg Empire..." the verbal fragments unspooled loonily. Habsburg? Ah, yes! It was here at Columbia—right here, he was almost sure of it, in Room 104—where Austria-Hungary, End of Empire and Republican Aftermath had met. The David of thirty years past, autumn 1979, was a hairier animal, a senior, and an uncritical admirer of Evelyn Waugh and Terry Southern. His professor was a flamboyant bald dandy named Raimund. "Cafes ... casual intercourse ... thriving Jewry ... toleration ... tragedy." So very many hours of notetaking, so much intense Socratic thrust-and-parry, not to be able to dredge up better than these hackneyed bites! They ran across his mind's screen as a droll head loomed stagily above, a fierce and cerebral signifier of pre-Anschluss Vienna. This surreal scrap, and no more, was all David had retained of the cosmopolitan capital: a head. The contextual body of facts and characters was gone. The passage of time, David gloomily reflected, could be illustrated by an infinite progression of nested heads, Karl Popper's in Raimund's, Raimund's in Semple's, Semple's into yet someone else's, objects physically observable and imposing shrinking to feebly firing chemicals. David felt young, residually. He did not want to be in the position of a killjoy Old Testament prophet, bearing stern witness to a passed age—didn't really want to think of it as passed. Yet, undeniably, the fat fingers that had singled out raised hands and etched tiny but potent marks (typically "B-") on David's history exams were now ash-fragile tendrils on a dumb corpse; the dear old professor's theater of engagement had fallen to others to command.

The man now facing Room 104 was a torch carrier for midlist fiction, subcategory social satire, and was intellectually formed when such things were worldly forces. His hair, still brown with little gray, was cut short but otherwise as unkempt as in '79. His present audience's average age appeared about nineteen (though a few others had evidently spotted the single nine-point sentence in the New Yorker listings and made their way uptown). This would seem to be an unlikely readership for *Class Dismissed*, the latest of his comically underselling novels. Maybe they had been forced by some obscure mechanism to attend. For whatever reason they had come, they were surely patient, as they had now waited for nearly a full minute for David to answer a question, which, in the course of his depressive Austrian interlude, he had forgotten.

"I'm sorry, the question once again please?"

The young lady with red-framed eyeglasses and black hair, liquidly shimmering like molten glass and pulled tightly back, smiled. "I was asking about Chuck," she said. "We see everything in *Class Dismissed* through his eyes, right? He comes to New York as a schoolteacher from small-town Arkansas, a little naïve and a bit, I don't know...dull, next to some of the more badly behaving characters? I mean, I liked him, but wasn't he dull, in a likeable way? I guess I couldn't quite get my head around him." She shifted her weight from one leg to the other. "And I kind of wondered if he was basically David Semple." A ripple of laughter rewarded her insouciance. Though her words and her tone were unobjectionable enough, David instantly disliked her—frames, speech, stance, self-assurance—disliked, to be fair, her whole generation, all those yakking fresh-faced little slacker-strivers, bogus bohemians, shallowly literate speed-readers. Her question in its first version had used about a dozen words. Now she was lolling about in the limelight, casting fumbling aspersions on his technical competency.

"I'd like to hear your thoughts on this...device, the good-guy narrator," she continued. "Chuck has to compete with some pretty sharp characters. Maude, the lesbian adoptive mother of the autistic girl. Kirby, the janitor. Roger Pettigrew, the securities analyst who gets fellated by his personal trainer during that wonderful houseboat party scene." Another ripple. "With such a colorful panorama, why have Chuck be the lens? Why have him at all? Would the satire have played differently in the third-person omniscient?"

David set his jaw. The girl's commentary was smart enough, even penetrating, in its way. It merited nothing less than a smooth and total evasion. "One manifest danger of the squeaky-clean narrator," said David, giving "manifest" a slightly morbid weight and tapping his pencil in play with the dactylic lilt of his phrases, "is that he may bore the reader. He may indeed earn our detestation. Most fatally, we may be unconvinced of his humanity. Who is Nick Carraway?" The tone of the question and the beat that followed created a moment of doubt as to its rhetorical intent, during which the girl blanched and sat down. "An everyman for all ages? Or a product of his particular biography, Minnesota and Yale and so on? A complex of mixed motives, an easygoing cipher? Gatsby's dupe? Some of all of the above? And what does it say, that this discussion over such . . . seemingly elemental distinctions . . . does not abate, all these years later?"

David smiled generously and looked around. Way back in his palate, near his tonsils, a little hammer was pinging: he was getting thirsty, and must get this Q&A over with and a long night of narcosis started. But he wished to leave an impression of fundamental seriousness, not blow job on a boat, in the air behind him, and so onward his little speedboat of pontification lurched. "It says that our straight man, he who tells our story, need not be a carelessly deployed device, much less simply the author in disguise. Further, it reminds us, as any book worthy of its two hard covers reminds us, that the reader bears the responsibility of serious engagement. She—" David held the girl's eyes firmly, his pronoun underscoring both his easygoing progressivism and her vagina—"owes the characters more than 'like/don't like,' as though she's, ahem, in high school with the characters. Mere likeability, in literature as in life"—the inchoately rising epigram now signaled the advent of land—"does not, in the long run, ahem, sustain or suffice."

David brought his hands to rest on the table. His answer had addressed questions no one in this room had asked, or possibly would ask, in any room, ever. But it did sidestep a blunt admission such as, "After twenty-seven years of tireless effort I have absorbed a little of Dawn Powell's technique and none of her genius." It also served in its elegance to shame the slovenly speech of his inquisitor. "If there are no more questions," said David, graciously, "I thank you for your time, ladies and gentlemen."

He had parked his rental car at 113th and Amsterdam. On the way there from campus he dialed his hotel on his BlackBerry—a just-purchased gadget, its tiny raised keypad numbers put him in mind of cell inflammation, and were constantly foiling his fingers and eyes—and was irritated to be told that its bar closed at 10 PM. An hour from now: hardly enough time to drive all the way to the East 30s and plea-bargain a spot in the overcrowded parking garage. A plan B would have to be improvised. Preferably one which didn't involve a tipsy crosstown excursion later in the night. But only preferably.

Here on upper Broadway the traffic seemed to flow a little less manically than, say, in midtown, where taxis turning onto east-west streets tended to brake inches short of baby strollers and the commercial imperative dictated the tempo. On either side of the street, there were few remnants of David's undergrad days. A bookstore at 114th still hawked left-ish paranoia, but was now called Morningside Books rather than Papyrus. The jazz bar known as the West End had been shuttered long ago. "Koch... Abzug...Roszak...Thalia (smoking in back section only!)... Margot." David bought a slice at a walk-up counter and continued south. At the window of a casual clothing retailer, he paused, chewing and regarding a polo shirt, electrically striped blue and yellow. The store was part of a chain that was in malls back home in Little Rock. Here the window display was brighter, more sumptuous. The tones made David imagine a top-secret Eastman Lab method by which Partridge Family negatives were treated to look as though shot on a digital camcorder. "Margot," he said aloud, experimentally. He tossed his crust in a can and lit a Winston.

Like his campus, he knew, his city had disappeared since he had moved to Arkansas in 1985 to marry Joan. That city was the bad old New York: festering, fluorescent, nonworking, bankrupt and scarcely governable, God-baiting, drugged, un-American, scabrous, sensation-mad. To those who had braved it, this New York had seemed, for all its teetering on ruin, a rude and irreversible reality. And yet in a geological blink it had gone away, been buried as completely as Tikal or Tenochtitlan. Like the replacement of Aztec folkways by European civilization, this was probably a net plus. But, if the law of energy conservation held, those solid bodies must be somewhere—all their words and waste, desires and crimes, the buzzing plasma-light emanations of their wills to survive, prosper, argue, copulate, drink, destroy, reshape, ridicule. The more David dwelled on it the more certain he was that beneath all this shiny niceness and plutocratic vigor lurked something sinister and Manchurian. If a madman had annexed and cleansed the island, things couldn't have turned out much different.

He turned left off Broadway at 113th. Here there used to be a basement-level dive called Conaghan's, and David warmed when he saw that a bar still operated in the space. Descending the concrete steps and entering the inky darkness, he jumped as a figure suddenly at his right touched his arm.

"Sorry," said the figure, a heavy-lidded kid of about six feet. "You gotta put that out."

"Oh—no, I'm sorry," said David, and flicked his cigarette out the door behind him. Habit. You could still light up all you liked in the bars back on 3rd Street, where he still killed some off-hours (okay, since his divorce, a lot of off-hours), but smoking, by which one could formerly project sophistication, was now the pastime of diehards and hillbillies. David paid for a black and tan and sat down at a corner table.

The music, thank God, was familiar and not too loud—Lou Reed's "Walk on the Wild Side"—and the place only half-full.

David sipped his drink and strained his eyes across the room, in the direction of a four-for-a-quarter photo booth near the bar, as though to make something out—the name on a microbrewery bottle, a friend he was expecting. He fished his BlackBerry from the inside pocket of his jacket and laid it flat before him. There must be some kind of work he could appear busy at. He checked his e-mail box; no fresh arrivals. He clicked on the green picture of a handset—a handset? Wasn't that about as intelligible anymore as a reel-to-reel tape deck?—and was mortified to see his ex-wife's name, in four identical rows, topping the list of calls most recently made. "Joan...Joan...Joan...Joan." He had learned the phone's features well enough to save names to speed dial, but not well enough to activate the lock that kept buttons accidentally pushed during on-person storage from calling those you least wanted to talk to. Maybe he had pressed against the table at a funny angle, staring out that goddamned window at Hamilton. Maybe she'd sat and listened while he'd jabbered about Nick Carraway. Doubly sickening.

His black and tan drained, he rose and went for another. The bartender was pouring two drinks at once, with either hand, back turned. For the second time a hand fell on David's right arm.

"Drink alone often?" The speaker's eyes sparkled companionably behind the red frames. Beside her was a man about thirty, with a sharp small nose and thin, kinky hair.

"Yep," said David. "Doctor's orders."

"I might have guessed Arkansas was on the leading edge of alternative treatment," she laughed. "I'm Ava Gold, by the way. This is my friend Max. Max, this is the awesomely funny man we were just discussing."

"Of course," he said primly, shaking David's hand. "Outed by the ever-ready wit."

"I was telling him what a great job you did tonight—oh, thanks." Two clear drinks in outlandishly tall glasses had been placed before them. Ava fished a credit card out of a green cloth clutch. "David, won't you have one with us? I owe you at least that, after the ridiculous question I inflicted on you."

"Certainly, thank you," said David, who, for all that he felt about strangers in general and this one in particular, felt refreshed to be lifted from his ruinous thoughts by a woman, no less by one who—he could see better now that she was close—was pretty. Instinctively he emended his account of their earlier exchange. They had been performers in a public ritual...she had been thrown off her game by his long silence...or by his very presence!...they both deserved a redo. Oddly, her diction, here in the more relaxed setting, had undergone a change—she had gained in concision. Also there were her breasts. Under her fuzzy sweater they stood like welcoming pylons at an Egyptian temple. "Another black and tan," David told the bartender.

"I was telling Max," said Ava, "your answers seemed fully prepared, yet not stale from repetition. It's rare to find someone who can both write and perform. I've been to plenty of author events."

"As have I," said David.

"I'm sure it must be tiresome, getting the same questions all the time," said Max. His tone verged on acid condescension, and he spoke loudly but without visible exertion. David looked at his suit, the cut, texture, the fit around the shoulders. "Four thousand dollars," said the suit, but quietly.

"No, coal mining is tiresome," David said. "A book tour's a picnic."

"The fans are the ants?" said Max.

"Not nearly so numerous," said David. "I'd say that getting out and promoting your writing is character building, in theory. In practice, it probably neither builds nor damages. It's a job to be done, plain and simple."

"Sure," nodded Max. They had returned from the bar to a table next to the one David had occupied alone. Max took Ava's coat and handbag and put them with his trench jacket and briefcase on the empty fourth chair. "So, how long have they got you out for?" he asked as they settled in.

"Oh, ten days. Let's see, Barnes and Noble in Hoboken yesterday, tomorrow Albany. An independent seller called All the World's a Page."

"Ha!" said Max. "That's fruity. No wonder small bookstores are going the way of, um, Albany."

"Where are you staying?" said Ava with deliberate casualness. "I bet they put you someplace cool—the Waldorf? The W?"

David broadened a small reflexive grimace into a contortion of his lower face, baring his gums as he conceived a dodge. "There is no 'they,'" he said. "No travel agents, no groomers, no satraps." He swallowed a third of his glass. "I'm down in Battery Park, third bench from the water. What about you, anyway, what's your line?"

"Ha," said Max again, bitterly. "Don't ask. I'm a faceless cog at a biotech company in Jersey City. Senior Trainer. A glorified salesman, is what it really amounts to."

"What did Golda Meir say?" said Ava. "'Don't be so modest, you're not that great.'" To David she explained, "Max is no cog. He's well-respected in immunology."

"That's commendable," said David.

"Yeah," said Max. "Call me when you're ready to trade jobs."

"And you?" David said to Ava.

"Ava here," said Max, patting her arm, "though she'd never say as much to you, is one hell of a writer."

"Oh?" said David.

"I have a website," conceded Ava. "And I do little memoirish things. I'm trying to combine some of them and turn them into a novel. I mean, it's fun for me. I wouldn't sit here with David Semple and say another word about it. Jeez, you'd think I was obsessed if you knew how long I've been reading you! My favorite is *Wanton Physics*."

"That was 1990," said David, banging the bottom of his empty glass softly from side to side, like an orphan. "Your memoirs, what are they? Comic, therapeutic, falsehoods?"

"Oh, don't feel obligated to ask."

"No, I'm sincerely interested." He hoped he sounded it.

"I have a couple of her pieces here in my briefcase," said Max, touching it. "As it happens. Ava is terrible at self-promotion. That's one thing you could help her with. Hey, buddy, how about another black and tan?"

"And a glass of Maker's, neat, if you don't mind," said David.

Max glided away, and Ava squeaked her chair a couple inches nearer David's. "I have a feeling I came off the wrong way back at Hamilton," she said. "Accusatory."

"Did you really think Chuck was dull?"

"I liked him," insisted Ava. "But I—oops! I forgot."

"Oh, please," said David. "Don't hold me to some...orotund pronouncement I pulled out of my ass at a reading. I'm like anyone, making it up as I go. Who knows what makes good writing?" He circled the rim of his glass with his index finger. "I'm just a salesman, like...your friend."

"He's not himself tonight," said Ava. "I'm not sure why. Maybe two writers at the same table is too much for him. Max is a frustrated creative type." She turned her head to make sure he wasn't approaching, and David leaned his closer in case a confidence was coming. "We met in a Russian literature class, actually, at City College. He was two years ahead of me. Even though I stayed in the world of books more than him, Max has always been the creative one."

Two "c"-words was too many for David, and he pulled back, slouching lower in his chair. "Creative is overrated," he told her firmly. "So he doesn't sit around in a garret making up stories, eating pretzels, getting drunk. He's got a job. He's contributing a little something to society. A trick your average navel-gazing pretzel eater can't seem to pull off." Though he didn't care to defend Max, and didn't exactly subscribe to these reactionary sentiments, venting them at the girl was too satisfying to resist.

"Well, he appreciates good literature, anyway, and so do I," said Ava cautiously. "That's why we came to see you."

"Sure. Listen, I'm not calling you a pretzel eater."

"I've been called—well, I don't even know what that means," said Ava.

"Cheap and insubstantial," explained David. "I get the feeling you're not."

"Gee, thanks," laughed Ava.

"So," David took a deep breath, "how about those stories of yours?"

"I could send you away with a copy of one I just finished," said Ava, nodding at the horrifyingly thick-looking briefcase. "That is, I think it's finished—it felt that way last week. You'll have to let me know." She spoke faster. "It's about this couple— they have this on-again, off-again relationship. He works for Morgan Stanley and she's torn between him and this handsome guitar player who lives in Williamsburg. I'm not sure I got some of the financial-type details just right. And the opening scene might—it could probably be tighter. If you read it, you have to promise not to be put off by it right away." She seemed fastened on him; he was slipping away. "The meat of it is really the characters, their relationship, and once a couple establishing details are out of the way, it sort of gets rolling, I think."

David nodded blankly. "Don't let me leave without it," he said.

"You'll give me your honest impression, won't you? I don't bruise easy."

"Yeah...no, I absolutely would not give you my honest impression. If it's bad, I won't say, and either way, you shouldn't make any changes based on my reaction." Having used this last sentence on other occasions, he was speaking while thinking along completely unrelated lines: Where was that guy with the beer? Why had it grown so ungodly loud in here?

"What are you working on now?" said Ava. If he had been listening he would have bridled at the collegial presumption. What was that noise? It was music, some kind of British proto-punk, and was easily five times louder and harsher than the previous song, both in speaker output and performance. The room had filled in considerably, and the bar was jammed solid on all sides. Max was nowhere visible.

"Are you working on something?" Ava said. David was some distance away, conducting a kind of reconnaissance, observing the room—its footprint, furnishings, distributed contents—as from a spy satellite, a grainy rendering of suspect dark surfaces and booby-trap-laden potentialities. Coldly noting his position on the sidelines, he saw that he, David Semple, was about to enter a humiliating battle, motivated by—What? Some tired, vestigial idea of gamesmanship?—and in pursuit of an object that held no clear interest of its own. He would have to contrive a mannerly exit for himself, or else allow things to meander on uncertainly. He returned his focus to Ava, who was regarding him with concern.

"I am working on something," he said, "called Is Max Presently Fucking You?"

It was a gambit, he figured, that would speed the course one way or the other. But Ava paused, with her mouth open, and in the next moment Max re-emerged, out of the raucous sea.

"Hey, kids—Noah's Alcoholic Ark!" he announced, setting two glasses, one large and one small, in front of each of them and taking his chair.

"Excuse me?" said Ava.

"No," said David, tossing back half the tall glass and all of the short one, and rising with a courtly flourish. "Excuse me." He elbowed a path through the throng, toward the men's room. Near the far end of the bar he snuck a backward glance at his table. There on his vacated chair was his brown jacket. But it was not cold outside, and as long as he had his BlackBerry—he touched his shirt pocket—the jacket seemed a not-too-painful sacrifice. He crossed to the other side of the bartender's island, where he presumed Max had been swallowed, and walked the length bent forward and head down. Near the end there was an empty stool in front of an unfinished bottle of Red Stripe and a plate waiting to be bussed. He swigged the beer, stuffed a few cold French fries into his mouth, and ducked out the door.

As the cab swung off Amsterdam into Central Park, premonitions of sinister forces returned. A thickly forested expanse of land was, back in Arkansas, a natural paradise perfect for fishing and wandering. Here, it was a public-works project ideal for concealing sex crimes. A cab in the oncoming lane, headlights blazing, charged around a curve at them like a leopard. Dank nineteenth-century tunnels of uncertain utility branched byzantinely under the earth. Maybe the thousands of homeless who formerly swarmed the sidewalks were kept down there. A twinkle of museums and townhouses rose over the treeline. Leaving the park and turning onto Fifth felt like a release into fresh air.

"Ava Gold writer": working with one finger on the tiny keypad he entered the phrase into the Google box on his BlackBerry. The gray bar grew, and his loins shifted queasily; the illicit request had an uncontrollable momentum, like a Ouija planchette. A fresh screen displayed his command on the top line and a block of type below, headed by a link, "Ava's TypePad Weblog," in blue and underscored. "Recent comments...about me... miscellany...writer sightings...Joy Williams has never been a stranger to controversy..." David scowled, clicked the red handset button three times quickly, and returned his vision outward. A hulking condominium, mid-construction, paralyzed by scaffolding, appeared on his left. "Homeless...needles...rent control..." came the crawl across the bottom of his mind's frame. "Empyrean...necktie...Stratford Steakhouse...Margot." All

Margot. He did not take a sentimental glance west-
ing 49th. Yet the awareness that he had resisted looked. Her apartment had been on a terrible block, in a
ory brick building eaten away by vermin and neglect, all
ay out in the no-man's land of West Ninth. Leaving there
one early morning, he saw a man shot from a fast-moving Chevy
Impala. The victim ran howling and holding his arm around the
corner and out of sight; the car squealed off toward the river.
Absurdly destructive drugs were just about routine, those days.
Why, you couldn't open a book or go to a film without seeing
them—couldn't avoid them in any social circle of conceivable
interest—couldn't walk down any street confident of not being
shot. It was hard to imagine, or explain.

At 48th the driver turned east and then continued down
Lexington. Pay phones: the modernistic hair-dryer-like instal-
lations had littered the landscape in the pre-BlackBerry eighties. There, just north of Grand Central Station, David, a brown
wrapped bundle gripped tight under his arm, had called Irwin
Shaw, who was an hour late for lunch. The old writer was probably still stuck at George's place, David guessed, bickering over
his subsidiary-rights split. Ring, click, and—there he was, Irwin
Shaw, in sober, watch-ticking, nonfictional reality, audible over
the noise of the trains and the taxis and the falafel stands, a
live voice on a handset manufactured by Western Electric, as
yet undivested of the almighty American Telephone and Tele-
graph Corporation, blurting gravelly monosyllables into David's
ear even as Margot was at her desk two miles away, doing her
noble work, helping the indigent find housing, laboring to ame-
liorate others' poverty while blithely sealing hers, content not
only in her nobility but in her virginal mobility—Twenty-three!
Untethered! Away for good from Shaker Heights!—and chat-
ting excitedly on another of AT&T's signaling units with Chet,
a pockmark-faced lawyer who did pro bono work for Hope
House, a staunchly irony-deaf man who could entertain with a

straight face all the drippy, earth-hugging cant—"social justice
...disenfranchised...restoring hope"—that made David's eyes
roll, a man who could easily defer gratifications—certain of
them—such as shambling whiskey-laced lunch meetings late
into the afternoon with novelists of the forties (the men David
worked with were exuberantly profane, in the aggregate, jowly,
pink-faced, cragged but somehow boyish), these old lions who
had been dropped by Knopf or Random House to land at
places like Empyrean, where their late-period efforts gathered
dust on stockroom shelves, except for the copies pilfered by
young editors for their girlfriends...and there he was, David,
down into Grand Central and headed to Times Square Station,
speeding on underground tracks into that sleazy sinkhole, the
west-side enantiomorph of the palatial Beaux Arts depot of the
east with its great four-faced clock and its broad stairway up to
Lexington where each weekday for four years he emerged duti-
fully if blearily into the nine o'clock sunlight, little suspecting
how fast, against the deceptive meandering quality of the day-
to-day, Joan and Little Rock were closing in...and there she
was, Margot, as he swung open the door on Ninth Avenue (his
own key), twenty-three and beautiful, sitting by the iron-grat-
ed window lost in *Apes of God*, hair black and shoulder-length
and unbrushed, eyes looking up and softening as he opened
the brown bundle—Shaw's galleys and some other hardbound
new titles—a terrible parting gift, but then he hadn't known it
was that.

Passed out in his hotel bed, the ventilation hissing and
groaning, a dream came to David in which he sat at a table in a
dark steakhouse. Facing him was Irwin Shaw. But Shaw was in
the dream a young man, clear-eyed and on top of his game, and
David was the elder by several decades. Despite this age flip-
flop, the mentor-protégé dynamic was unaltered.

"It disturbs me that all these human beings should vanish,"
David said, simply.

"They're there," said Irwin softly. "Just not as far as you know."

"What's the difference?" David despaired. "I can't follow the thread anymore. It's like a story without a beginning or an end, only a middle. Things accumulating without sense...people wandering in and out..."

"You might have too many characters," Irwin shrugged. "Who is this Max?"

David frowned. "He's the new New York. You don't know what it's like since you left. It's all big money, swagger, and glitter. No ideas, no fun. No subversion."

Shaw's neck was growing rubbery. A tumor in the shape of a small mushroom was pressing nearly through the skin, and his nostrils hissed. "You could have had the girl," he declared. "You could be fucking her now!" He stabbed a wedge of steak fiercely with his fork.

"Yes, but..." David trembled as he felt the maudlin words gather in his brain and spill from his mouth. "I've only ever loved one woman. And that was so long ago...I'm not sure it ever actually happened."

Again Irwin shrugged. Then he listed theatrically onto one buttock, grimaced, and farted loudly. The sound, startling as a thunderclap, woke David. It was ten o'clock. He sat upright in the bed and saw himself in the mirror, puffy and still wearing last night's shirt. Heart thumping, he patted the front pocket: empty. He cursed aloud and sprang up, hastily combing the floor and furniture tops, as his brain lumbered to arrange recent scenes and events in their proper order. The taxi—he had had the BlackBerry in the taxi. That was where it was. And, since he couldn't remember any detail about the vehicle...Well, there was a story with an end, wasn't it. Careful what you say in dreams, he told himself grimly.

Downstairs he accessed his email from the hotel computer and printed out the details of his Albany appearance that afternoon. Wheeling his suitcase behind him, he walked north to Grand Central, took the shuttle to Times Square, switched to the number 1 uptown, and returned aboveground at Cathedral Parkway. Upon returning to his rental car, he was startled to see that he had absently left all four doors unlocked. In the back seat was a shoulder bag with some magazines, flight itineraries, and $150 dollars in cash. In the front passenger were an atlas, pretzels, an iPod, and a liter of Coke. Nothing had been disturbed.

Humanesque

★

BY BEN WEAVER

The streets are quiet at the end of summer. The hottest days have passed. Soon the trees will burst into colors of flame and it will be dark by dinnertime.The town is on the water. All roads lead to the sea.

Shortly after four in the morning he walks from the bedroom down the hall to the darkened bathroom. Lifting the seat, he judges his aim by the sound of urine hitting toilet water. Then he puts the seat down and returns to the bedroom without flushing.

He pulls the sheet up over himself leaving the top third of his body exposed. Steadily, she breathes next to him. Her back is turned. She sleeps without a shirt.

There is a church across the road. Tall lights stand in the parking lot and loom over the blacktop like giant sunflowers. Their light bleeds into the bedroom through a space in the curtains where the hems fail to meet.

He lies on his back, unable to sleep.

Thoughts roll around in the space behind his eyes.

Curling his toes under the sheet he watches the shadows move on the wall. The two rooms down the hall are empty. His daughters have grown up. One married, the other divorced. Both have their own families, their own homes.

The air smells of eucalyptus.

Sitting up he swings his legs over the side of the bed. His left foot catches one of the curtains and widens the space between them, letting more light in. It spreads to her turned back. His eyes pass over the tan lines, the few scattered freckles, then down to the stretch marks that disappear under the waistband of her underwear. His eyes linger there.

In the dark he finds a shirt and pulls it over his head. With his left arm stretched winglike to the side, his fingers run along the wall as he walks down the hall past the bathroom and living room, into the widening blackness of the kitchen. He flips the light switch and the darkness goes away.

He takes a glass down from the cupboard, turns on the tap, and fills it. He stands at the sink drinking. There is a puddle of rainwater in the windowsill. He pours out the remaining contents of the glass and listens while it twists down the drain.

He built the house. He could have hired a builder who would have finished in half the time. But he wanted to touch everything himself, the nails, the plywood, the cement block. He did not want to live in a house whose walls held the history of anyone other than that of his family.

They moved in on an autumn day. The wind disassembling leaves from the trees and scattering them across the sidewalks and streets like loose leaf-paper. He felt warm, contemplative, and filled with a great sense of accomplishment. Tonight a similar wind is pushing at the trees, making shadows on the houses like wolves fleeing fire. He stands with one hand on the scarred countertop, staring into the knife marks, the black hashes crisscrossing its wooden surface. Miniature canyons dammed with vegetable dirt, bacon grease, and skin, physical evidence of passing time.

He considers himself fortunate and with age feels blessed. He is healthy and so is his family. He has few regrets. Unhappy or complicated times have been rare in his life. Recalling moments from his past brings satisfaction. He imagines his memories as a collection of butterflies, named and categorized with pinned wings, preserved under glass. They are his life and he holds them dear.

His hand follows the countertop to a spot near the stove. Five russet potatoes sit in an earthenware bowl she made in college. There is a faint smell of dish soap and skin moisturizer.

The kitchen begins to move, to transform itself like a stage set, everything on wheels rolled to the side. His two daughters appear in the kitchen. They are eight and eleven. Their hair is the color of sunset. They are standing on a wooden chair next to their mother peeling potatoes, letting the skins fall into the sink. He was standing exactly where he is now.

His oldest daughter had been to the orthodontist that afternoon to have braces put on. Her lips were shredded and dry, scattered with specks of blood. They looked separate from the rest of her face. He felt powerless. He no longer had the same ability to soothe her pain that he had when she was a child, when simply being her father was enough. He could see how youth was falling behind her; she was rapidly approaching womanhood, becoming an individual, like a vine growing away from the fence post directly into the sun.

He can hear their laughter. It mixes with the wind in the trees outside, the smell of their skin fresh as spilt milk. He whispers their names. It is all he can do.

On the horizon, lights from the car dealership near the highway make a white hole in the night like the pictures he's seen on TV of UFOs. Sometimes he thinks of loading his .22 and driving over to the dealership. He imagines taking a picture of the sky before and one after he shoots out all the lights.

Standing at the patio door he presses his fingers into the screen. Little black dots, mosquitoes and moths, buzz and dart, occasionally landing on it, drawn by the warm air and light from inside. Pushing the door open he steps out onto the cement. The air is thick and carries a heavy scent. The hair on his arms stands up. The wind nips the top of one ear.

Looking across the backyards, he sees no lighted windows. His breath is the loudest noise. A rabbit makes a diagonal across the yard and disappears into the bushes at the back. The clothes she washed the afternoon before are still hanging on the line. Dry now, they blow in the wind like telltales.

The hottest summer he can remember was the one just before his youngest daughter started the first grade. Night after night the heat woke him, and he lay twisted in sweaty sheets unable to sleep.

In the middle of one such night he rose from bed and navigated his way through the house without turning on any lights. He was going to sit for a while on the back steps, in the cooler air. Approaching the screen door he noticed something moving in the yard, a blur. He nearly stopped breathing. His hand went to his eyes to make sure they were in fact open and he wasn't dreaming.

In the garden stood a mother elephant and her baby.

He watched in awe, their trunks rising and lowering, pulling tomatoes from the vines. They were massive yet startlingly silent, like sky cranes seen from a car window, hoisting steel in the distance over an approaching skyline.

He woke his daughters and carried them to the back door in their white, wrinkled nightgowns. They didn't say a word. They just stood there with their mouths open rubbing their eyes and watching.

In the morning at breakfast, both girls said they had dreamt of elephants. He tried to explain. He showed them the trampled garden. In fact the circus was in town. The elephants had escaped. They thought he was teasing. Even now as grown women when he tells the story they don't believe him.

Stepping off the cement steps into the dewy grass, he walks to the clothesline and begins unpinning the clothes.

His skiff is up on its trailer under a blue tarp along the fence. It rests there like an unlit log on the grate of a fireplace. In the middle of the tarp, a puddle of rainwater littered with pine needles and a few oak seeds holds the moon.

They used to take the boat out fishing with friends on the weekends. She would pack lunches. They would get sunburned. Drink beers. It never mattered if they caught any fish or not. That felt like a long time ago.

The air goes in and out of his lungs, his heart working gently with his blood. He takes down the last piece of laundry, a white dress she wears over her bathing suit when she goes to the beach. He folds it and places it in the basket with the rest of the laundry and walks toward the fence that separates his yard from the neighbor's.

He rests both hands on the pointy cedar pickets. They are sharp against his palms. There are two cars in the neighbor's driveway and a motorcycle pulled up farther on the grass beside the house.

Yesterday afternoon he went to the grocery store. He decided to take a different way home than the way he usually went. The sky was clean and bright. A motorcycle passed him in the left lane. A woman was riding on the back, her arms around the man driving. She was wearing shorts. Her legs glistened and reflected the sun like a long fish on a stringer pulled up from water.

He imagined their life, their morning. The man was her husband. After breakfast she had taken a shower, sitting down in the tub, the showerhead pointing at the tiles while she scraped the tiny hairs and foam from her legs. He had come into the bathroom to brush his teeth and through the shower curtain they talked and decided to take a ride. It was a beautiful day.

A few minutes after the motorcycle passed, traffic came to a sudden halt. The truck in front of him stopped so abruptly that he nearly rear-ended it.

Several cars ahead merged out of the way. He saw the motorcycle on its side. The man who had been driving was kneeling next to the woman. She was motionless on her back beside the bike.

For a moment he forgot he was on the highway. Lost, he watched as the man extended his hand and placed it on the woman's neck. Everything was moving fast, though nothing was moving at all. In a sudden burst the man fell straight backward, as though a giant invisible hand had swatted him away from something it wanted to grasp. He didn't move again.

Someone was on a phone calling for help. There wasn't anything he could do.

All the way home he thought about the man. When he had touched the woman's neck, had he found no pulse? Was that the reason he had fallen over backward so dramatically, so suddenly? Was she dead?

Turning his head from the neighbor's yard he looks back at his house, the light in the kitchen reaching through the screen door and fading out across the patio. He starts back. Before going inside he stands on the cement steps and listens. There are sea birds in the distance, the sound of halyards hitting against masts making a faint ring, and the highway growing louder.

Inside he walks through the kitchen and switches off the light. His feet leave a moist print on the linoleum floor with a dry space in the middle where his arch fails to touch.

She is still sleeping. Sitting down on the bedside he wipes his bare feet on the carpet. A few blades of grass fall in amidst the twists of polyester. He pulls off his shirt and lies on his side facing her back. He touches her shoulder, feeling the pressure of her body against his hand as she breathes. He hasn't told her about the accident. She doesn't know he wakes up like this. The light outside is rising. The days are countable.

Robbie Fulks (Chicago, IL)

Robbie Fulks is a long time Chicago resident whose musical career spans twenty years and an eclectic range of songwriting that reflects his own unique take on country music. In addition to his solo work, he produced a tribute to Johnny Paycheck, *Touch My Heart* that made several of the year's best-of lists. His most recent release is *Revenge!* (Yep Roc Records), a double live CD. He is a contributor to the 2008 book *A Guitar and a Pen*, (Center Street).

Mary Gauthier (Baton Rouge, LA)

Mary Gauthier was born in New Orleans and began her career as a singer and songwriter at the age of 35, after owning and running several successful restaurants in Boston, MA. Her third album, *Filth and Fire,* was named indie CD of the year by Jon Pareles of the *New York Times.* Her first major label release, *Mercy Now,* was named to top 10 lists for the year 2005 in dozens of publications, including the *New York Times,* the *Los Angeles Times, New York Daily News,* and *Billboard Magazine.* In the same year, the Americana Music Association voted her "Best New Artist." Her second Universal/Lost Highway release, *Between Daylight and Dark,* was released in 2007.

Cynthia Hopkins (Brooklyn, NY)

Cynthia Hopkins is the recipient of the 2007 Alpert Award in Theatre, honoring her work as a writer, composer, musician, and performer of unique music/theater projects featuring her band, Gloria Deluxe. With Gloria Deluxe, Hopkins is currently at work on an album of love songs titled *LOVE is gonna be my weapon and YOU are gonna be my first victim.* With her ensemble company Accinosco, Hopkins is at work on a new performance piece titled *The Success of Failure (or, The Failure of Success).*

Cam King (Fredericksburg, TX)

Originally from Albuquerque, guitarist/songwriter Cam King has made his musical home in Austin, Los Angeles, Nashville, and now Fredericksburg, TX. Selections from his early music were used by Tobe Hooper, fresh from the movie *Texas Chainsaw Massacre*, for his follow-up film, *Bloodfest*. In 1978, Cam co-founded The Explosives, the Austin bandassociated with the legendary Roky Erickson. Cam's songs have been covered by Garth Brooks, Marcia Ball, Lonestar, and others. At home in the hill country and on the road, Cam performs, composes, and records. He writes prose and the occasional poem, but prefers prose for economic reasons—"Writing poetry generally takes acouple more beers than prose."

Damon Krukowski (Cambridge, MA)

Damon Krukowski has recorded over a dozen albums with the bands Damon & Naomi, Galaxie 500, and Magic Hour, and is the author of the poetry collection *The Memory Theater Burned* (Turtle Point, 2004). He and his partner Naomi Yang also run the publishing house Exact Change, in Cambridge, Massachusetts.

Jon Langford (Chicago, IL)

Jon Langford was a founding member of the punk band The Mekons. In the 1980s he began incorporating folk and country music into his other punk rock projects such as the Pine Valley Cosmonauts and the Waco Brothers. Langford is a respected visual artist represented by Yard Dog in Austin, TX. His multimedia music/spoken-word/video performance, *The Executioner's Last Songs*, premiered in 2005, and has been performed in several other cities. He illustrated the comic strip *Great Pop Things* under the pseudonym Chuck Death. He's a regular contributor to *This American Life*. *Nashville Radio*, a collection of his artwork and writings, was published in 2006.

Patty Larkin (Cape Cod, MA)

Patty Larkin is a multi-talented singer, songwriter, and guitarist. She has been a favorite for years in folk circles and in her home territory of New England where she has won seven Boston Music Awards including outstanding folk act, outstanding folk album, and outstanding song/songwriter. Her most recent CD is *Watch the Sky*, which she wrote, produced, engineered, and edited.

Maria McKee (Los Angeles, CA)

Singer and songwriter Maria McKee came to fame as the lead singer for the pioneering Americana band *Lone Justice* followed by a solo career that includes six critically acclaimed albums. *The Washington Post* called her "a fiery amalgam of Dusty Springfield, Emmylou Harris, and Connie Francis". Her songs have been covered by everyone from Bette Midler to the Dixie Chicks. Her most recent recording is *Maria McKee: Live at the BBC*.

Rhett Miller (New York, NY)

Rhett Miller has been the lead singer in the Old 97's for 15 years and is also a successful solo musician. One of his short stories was published in *McSweeney's Quarterly Concern* and another was included in an anthology of writers writing about songs called *Lit Riffs* (MTV Books). Rhett Miller's most recent release is *The Believer.*

David Olney (Nashville, TN)

David Olney's musical career spans four decades. Known for his intense live performances, Olney's intelligent compositions have been recorded by everyone from Emmylou Harris and Linda Ronstadt to Del McCoury and Lonnie Brooks. The late singer-songwriter Townes Van Zandt put Olney on his short list of favorite writers, alongside Mozart, Lightnin' Hopkins, and Bob Dylan. His current album release is *Live At Norm's River Road House, Vol.1.*

Zak Sally (Minneapolis, MN)

Zak Sally is the former bassist for the band Low. He has been creating comics since the early 1990's and formally started the publishing house La Mano Press in Minneapolis, MN in 2005. His most recent comic is *Sammy the Mouse* (Fantagraphics).

Chris Smither (Boston, MA)

Chris Smither is an acclaimed singer-songwriter, whose career spans 40 years, 12 albums, and three DVDs. He tours worldwide, performing at clubs, concert halls, and festivals. Smither's songs have appeared in various films and television shows, and have been covered by Bonnie Raitt, Emmylou Harris and Diana Krall, among others. In 2006, Smither contributed an essay entitled "Become A Parent" to the book *Sixty Things To Do When You Turn Sixty*. His most recent CD is *Leave the Light On* with a new recording scheduled for release in late 2009.

Rennie Sparks (Albuquerque, NM)

Rennie Sparks is the lyricist, banjo and bass player for The Handsome Family. Together with her husband Brett Sparks (who writes the music) they have released eight CDs. Their latest CD, *Honey Moon* is a collection of love songs that is romantic in the truest sense of the word—where the raptures of love tangle in green vines, drift across moonlit seas, and shimmer in the wings of crawling bugs. *Honey Moon* was written in celebration of the Sparks' twentieth year of marriage.

Laura Veirs (Seattle, WA)

Laura Veirs was born in 1973 in Colorado Springs, Colorado. She didn't get involved with music until college, where she studied geology and Mandarin Chinese. She joined an all-girl punk band before eventually developing an admiration for folk and country music. She released her self-titled debut in 1999. Since then she has recorded five albums and toured extensively. Her most recent album,*Saltbreakers*, includes songs inspired by A.S. Byatt's novel *Possession* and Jose Saramago's *Blindness*.

Ben Weaver (St. Paul, MN)

Ben Weaver is a writer, artist and musician. Larry Brown wrote, "Ben Weaver is the most exciting young songwriter I've come across, an American original whose voice and guitar are matched only by the power of his words." He has published two books of poetry *Hand Me Downs Can Be Haunted* and *The Talking Comes Later*. His most recent release is *The Ax in the Oak*.

Jim White (Athens, GA)

Jim White has worked as a taxi driver, professional surfer, fashion model, photographer, filmmaker, and musician. His first CD *Wrong-Eyed Jesus* appeared in 1997 on the label Luaka Bop; since then he has released five CDs that have been described as "outer space alternative country" and "hypnotic storytelling." His most recent CD is *Transnormal Skipperoo*.

ACKNOWLEDGMENTS

This book was made possible by all of our friends, family, and the musicians who participated in this book. Special thanks to Marcy Horwitz, Megan & Mac Plumstead, David & Derryle Berger, Howie Cohen, Rich Meier, Marty Kotler, Bert Jacobs, Steve Dickinson, Jane & Al Levitan, Sandy Peskin, Donna Packer & Ed Wilczynski, Meg Taradash, Sandra & Todd Smith, David Calvert, Marla Hoicowitz, Hans Weyendt, Brad Zellar, Jim Harris, Harley McIlrath, Eric Lorberer, Sheila Keenan, & Kevin Duggan, John Baynes, Michael Cashin, Lise Solomon, Terry Fernilough, Juliet Patterson, Stu Abraham, Roy Schonfeld, John Mesjak, Ted Seykora, Colin Fuller and Michael D'Agostini.

When Julie Schaper and Steven Horwitz are not listening to music, they're reading. Both have worked in publishing in one capacity or another for 20 years. Their first co-editing project was *Twin Cities Noir.* They live in St.Paul, MN with their two dogs.